CATLANTIS

CATLANTIS

ANNA STAROBINETS

Original Illustrations by
ANDRZEJ KLIMOWSKI

Translated from the
Russian by Jane Bugaeva

THE NEW YORK REVIEW CHILDREN'S COLLECTION
NEW YORK

THIS IS A NEW YORK REVIEW BOOK
PUBLISHED BY THE NEW YORK REVIEW OF BOOKS
435 Hudson Street, New York, NY 10014
www.nyrb.com

First published in Russian as *Котлантида*
This translation first published by Pushkin Press in 2015

The publication of the book was negotiated through
Banke, Goumen & Smirnova Literary Agency (www.bgs-agency.com)

ИНСТИТУТ ПЕРЕВОДА

AD VERBUM

*Published with the support of the
Institute for Literary Translation, Russia.*

Library of Congress Cataloging-in-Publication Data
Names: Starobinets, Anna, author. | Klimowski, Andrzej, illustrator. |
  Bugaeva, Jane, translator.
Title: Catlantis / by Anna Starobinets ; illustrations by Andrzej
  Klimowski ; translated by Jane Bugaeva.
Other titles: Kotlantida. English | New York Review children's
  collection.
Description: New York : New York Review Books, 2016. | Series: New
  York Review children's collection
Identifiers: LCCN 2016006943| ISBN 9781681370002 (alk. paper) |
  ISBN 9781681370026 (ebook)
Subjects: LCSH: Cats—Juvenile fiction. | Time travel—Juvenile
  fiction.
Classification: LCC PG3493.48.T369 K6813 2016 | DDC 891.73/5—
  dc23
LC record available at http://lccn.loc.gov/2016006943

ISBN 978-1-68137-000-2
Available as an electronic book; ISBN 978-1-68137-002-6

Cover design by Louise Fili Ltd.
Cover illustrations by Andrzej Klimowski
Text designed by Tetragon, London

Printed in the United States of America on acid-free paper.
10 9 8 7 6 5 4 3 2 1

CHAPTER 1

The Cat Everyone Respected

Baguette the cat liked to lie in the window and watch the birds. The birds were not afraid of him. First off, they had bird brains and always forgot that cats could hunt. Second off, during their more enlightened moments, they knew that Baguette was looking on them not as prey, but more from a philosophical point of view. He did not intend to attack them because the Petrov family, and Baguette was a part of this very family, lived on the twelfth floor of an apartment building. And so, the window in which Baguette was lying was also on the twelfth floor. Baguette was a very smart cat and had no intentions of jumping out of something that high up.

This particular double window had small square ventilation panes in its bottom right-hand corner. Mama liked to open them to let in the winter breeze, and it was precisely in this porthole that Baguette liked to lie. He always picked the most comfortable pose: his ginger tail hung inside the room, his whiskers poked outdoors and his downy belly was suspended in the six-inch gap between the two panes. So that he wouldn't fall out, all twenty of his claws dug tightly into the window frame.

"Oh, my!" Mama Petrov would yelp whenever she saw Baguette in this position. This time, she called out to her husband, "For God's sake, you've just got to put a screen in that window. Yes, darling, for the health and safety of our cat."

"A screen!" said Papa Petrov. "What kind of screen?"

"Oh, you know, the kind for flies and mosquitoes."

"For flies?" Papa frowned. "You mean the thin, synthetic kind...Am I understanding you correctly, darling?"

"Yes, darling."

"Hmm, I'll think about it...but first, have I understood you correctly? Do you have absolutely no respect for our cat?"

Mama bit her lip. This was quite an accusation. The thing is, everyone in the Petrov family—Mama, Papa, both grandmothers and grandfathers, the little girl Polina, her older brother Vadik and even the dog Bonehead—had great respect for Baguette ever since his heroic feat.

"You don't respect the cat who risked his life for our family?" continued Papa. "The cat who traveled from the past into the future and ventured into the Land of Good Girls? The cat who courageously fought an army of chiming clocks and rescued our beloved daughter Polina from that world of the past? How can you disrespect such a cat?!" For emphasis Papa would point at Baguette, who continued to sit nonchalantly in the open window, keeping a philosophical eye on the birds and pretending not to hear a thing.

"Why would you think that, darling?" Mama protested in a quivering voice. "I have the utmost respect for him."

"Well, then, explain to me how, my darling, how you can suggest this idea of a fly screen? How can you compare a cat to a fly?"

"But I wasn't—"

"An intelligent cat with a simple-minded fly! Do you really think that some thin screen is a match for our Baguette? You think he won't be able to tear it to pieces with his claws? Maybe you think he's going to beat his wings against it and buzz?!"

"You're absolutely right, my darling," Mama agreed. "A fly screen won't do at all. But we must think of his safety! Well, then, how about bars?"

"What?"

"Bars."

"Bars?" asked Papa. "Did you say bars? The metal kind?"

"Yes, darling, the metal kind. The kind you install for burglars and thieves."

"You mean like in prison?"

"Well, yes, but it's for his own good—for his health and safety!"

"I don't believe it!" Papa was now marching about the room. "So, you're saying that we have so little respect for our cat that we'll turn our house into a cat prison, *for his own good*? We're to imprison a free animal! We're to install the bars, humiliating this superhuman being in front of our neighbors, in front of his friends and acquaintances! Are you being serious?"

Baguette nervously swung his tail to the rhythm of Papa's speech. He was almost positive that the Petrovs would not install bars on the windows. Nonetheless, the possibility worried him, and even the smallest worry about this topic was enough to disturb his mental equilibrium. His fur would start molting then and there, and he would even feel the need to jump down from the window. In this state of imbalance, the cat had no business lying in an open window on the twelfth floor.

"Bars! Humiliating our cat in front of his beloved!" continued Papa.

"He's too young, he doesn't have a beloved," said Mama with little conviction.

"Well, I'm pretty sure he does," maintained Papa. "You still think of him as a kitten, but he's been a man for quite some time."

CHAPTER 2

Love and Bars

P apa was right: Baguette was in love. Her name was Purriana. She was slender and striped, her nose was as pink as a rosebud, her whiskers as white as snow on New Year's Day, and her coat shone like a diamond necklace. Every night Baguette would purrenade her from his window. Purriana loved the purrenades and she loved Baguette and ... and ... and she was a stray.

Which explains why Baguette was always so distressed when the Petrovs discussed window bars. There is nothing more embarrassing to an indoor house cat than to purrenade his beloved stray from behind bars!

"Who cares?" Bonehead the dog was surprised. "Bars or no bars, isn't it all the same? If she loves you, she won't even notice the bars."

"You're the only one who doesn't notice bars, Bonehead!" Baguette involuntarily let out his claws. "You don't even notice your own collar!"

"Hey, what's wrong with my collar?" Bonehead began twisting around trying to see his collar and its shortcomings.

"What's wrong with it?!" protested Baguette. "Why, if they tried to put a collar on me, I'd…well, I wouldn't allow that kind of embarrassment. I'd borrow your leash and do myself in straight away—with that very collar!"

"Why?"

"Because nothing matters more than freedom. I'm a free cat and—"

"If you're free, why don't you go outside, my friend?" Bonehead wondered. "Why do you stay here in captivity, eating our bread and—"

"I don't eat bread."

"You eat our fish and our chicken, you sleep in a human bed, you warm yourself by the radiator, you beg everyone to pet you—"

"I don't beg!"

"You let people scratch you behind your ears. Is that what you call freedom?"

"Yes, this is my kind of freedom," said Baguette with a frown. "A household freedom. But I won't allow it to be restricted by bars. If Purriana sees bars, she'll surely stop loving me. You have to understand, Bonehead, that it's all a question of status. Without bars you're a free house cat. You can purrenade your beloved through an open window and in doing so you offer her everything you enjoy yourself: the comfort of home, central heating, three daily meals, professional behind-the-ear massage, a clean litter box, clean sheets, vitamins for your fur, veterinary services—in a word, stability. But when you sing to her from behind bars you're offering her... well, you aren't offering her anything. She sees that you have no say in your own life and she chooses the street, she chooses the alley, she leaves. She leaves with the black cat Noir."

The black cat Noir was also a stray. He lived by the dumpster in the alley, hunted pigeons and ate scraps. Once he even ate a parakeet who stupidly flew out the window of a nearby apartment. Another time he caught and ate the neighbor's hamster—and both crimes remained unpunished. Everyone avoided Noir; they preferred to keep their distance from his dumpster. The fact of the matter was that Noir was not just a black cat, he was completely black, extremely black, as black as coal, there was not a single spot on his body that was not black—and cats like that were bad news.

"Polina, dear, please take out the trash. But don't go to the dumpster nearby, go to the other one," Mama would warn.

"But why?" Polina would ask. "The one nearby is nearby…"

"Yes, dear," Mama nodded sadly, "but there's a black cat there and he might cross your path!"

"So? Let him cross my path, I don't mind."

"No! It's bad luck if a black cat crosses your path."

"Why?"

"It's an omen."

"What's an omen?"

"Ah, an omen is a kind of law. A magical law."

"Well, then, why doesn't our president outlaw this silly law?"

"The president can't outlaw magical laws. He must obey them like everyone else."

"So the president is scared of black cats too?"

"Of course," nodded Mama. "Of course he is."

CHAPTER 3

The Engagement

Only extremely courageous people such as Papa Petrov dared to take the trash to the dumpster where Noir lived. Actually, even brave Papa Petrov only went there when accompanied by Bonehead. It usually went like this: Bonehead would growl to scare away Noir, Papa would quickly throw out the trash and the two of them would hurriedly flee this dangerous dumpster realm.

When they got back to their apartment building, they were greeted by Baguette's beloved Purriana. Bonehead never growled at her, but thats's not to say he liked her. To tell the truth, Bonehead did not share Baguette's tastes—Purriana seemed too spindly and secretive. No, he preferred Natasha, the neighbor's bulldog. She had a sturdy build and wore her heart on her sleeve. But Bonehead would never think to growl at his friend's beloved—he had too much respect for Baguette. So anytime he saw Purriana, he would politely wag his tail. Also, he helped the lovers communicate by passing notes between them. After all, how else can two cats in love communicate, when one is an indoor house cat and the other a stray street cat, if not by billets-doux.

Baguette's handwriting was large and masculine:

Precious Petite Purriana,

My love for you grows from day to day—it knows no bounds. Thus, I am unable to express my true feelings in prose and can do so only in poetry. To you, O Breathtaking Cat, I dedicate these lines:

I love you more than fish and even kitty chow.
I long to nuzzle the tip of your tail.
Without you my life is empty and dull.
Love comforteth, and love is all I hope for now.

Yours,
Baguette.

"Purr, purr, purr," answered Purriana in her elegant, fluttery handwriting. "Purr, purr, purr, purr, purr."

Near the end of winter, Baguette wrote to Purriana once more:

> *I love you more than life itself. I offer you my paw and heart. Be my wife.*

Then followed these lines of poetry:

> *I love you more than chicken, more than trout.*
> *I yearn to touch your tail, its playful tip,*
> *I yearn to kiss your lovely whiskered lips,*
> *And hour by hour my desire mounts.*

Purriana responded that very day:

> *Meow. I want you to know, my ginger darling, that you are not the first cat to offer me your paw and heart. Just yesterday, the black cat Noir asked me to be his wife.*

After this letter Baguette had a sleepless night (although he never really slept at night) and in the early morning he asked Bonehead to pass along this note:

Purriana, you're killing me! That black creature wants to marry you?! I can't even bear to hear his name! It makes my fur stand on end! Just the thought of him coming near you makes me spit and hiss. If you have agreed to marry him, know this: either he or I shall soon be fit for taxidermy, for I will challenge him to a duel! ~~My piercy claws will... My claws will piercingly...~~ *Either my claws will pierce his black heart or his claws will be the death of me. Period.*

Her response was reassuring:

How jealous you are, my ginger darling! How suspicious! How daring! I beg of you, do not torture yourself in vain—I have refused Noir. I coldly refused him. You, Baguette, are my only beloved ~~this moment... this month...~~*from now until forever. I will marry only you.*

The cat wedding was scheduled for the middle of spring.

CHAPTER 4

The Feat

According to the most ancient feline tradition, a male cat who intends to marry must, in honor of his beloved, accomplish a heroic feat.

At one time everyone took this tradition very seriously: cats would risk their lives to accomplish these lovers' feats. They would venture to the edge of the world, battle armies of plague-infested rats, journey across turbulent seas in the hulls of pirate ships, clamber up impossibly high cliffs, stir up revolutions, throw themselves into fires... but as centuries passed the feats grew more and more modest, the rats became healthier, the oceans less deep, the pirate ships more comfortable and the cliffs less steep. The tradition continued to weaken, until it became a mere formality. Nowadays it was enough for the groom to catch a small bird or mouse...

But for an indoor house cat even that could be a real challenge. What is a cat to do, unless his apartment is infested with mice and birds? Should he eat a pet hamster, who is actually a stand-up guy? Or better a parakeet, who is such a pleasure to chat with on long winter evenings? Hopeless situations like this are exactly what lead lovers to make rash decisions: cats jump from windows after sparrows, try to catch already poisoned cockroaches, fall into aquariums filled with goldfish...

Baguette did nothing of the sort. He sat in the open window, watched the birds with a philosophic eye and calmly awaited his wedding day.

"Hey lover-boy!" Noir yelled loudly from the street. "I hope you haven't forgotten about your feat! No feat—no Purriana! And she'll be all mine!"

Baguette wiggled his whiskers dismissively and said nothing.

Noir continued, laughing: "What're you even good for? A feat—as if! You're just a house cat. You're no better than a Pekinese... After all, you can't even catch a bird. Hey, Purriana, come here! Your beloved can't even catch a bird!"

"Oh, please," Baguette laughed into his whiskers. "What kind of idiot does he think I am? Does he think I'm going to jump to my death out of this twelfth-floor window? So that he can marry my Purriana? Wish on!"

"Go ahead, jump! Jump!" Noir didn't stop. "What about that feat! Look, a pigeon, a nice juicy pigeon! Can you catch him? You can't? Watch this then..." Noir jumped up and immediately caught the fat pigeon.

"Purriana!" he yelled in triumph, his black paw on the

pigeon's carcass. "Purriana, the cat of my dreams! Look, I just caught you a bird!"

Purriana, who was sitting nearby, gazed thoughtfully at Noir and his prey for a long time but stayed silent.

Baguette watched Noir from his window. His tail was twitching nervously but on the whole he remained calm. First of all, he knew that Purriana couldn't stand filthy dumpster pigeons (she had once written to him that she liked quail—and since there were no quail in their yard, he knew that Noir didn't stand a chance). And second of all, there was no need to bother about the feat because he had already accomplished one. Two winters ago, he had traveled from the past into the future, fought an army of chiming clocks, infiltrated into the Land of Good Girls and rescued Polina from that world of the past. Now that had been a real feat! Dumpster Noir could catch all the obese pigeons he wanted. Baguette was way above pigeon-catching—literally, from his twelfth-floor window.

Instead, he purrenaded Purriana from his window, ate his dinner, sang purrabies to the Petrovs and thought he had nothing to worry about.

He was wrong.

One March evening, when Noir had caught a particularly juicy pigeon and two sparrows to boot, Bonehead brought Baguette a letter from Purriana. The letter read:

My Dear Baguette,

Our wedding is scheduled for the middle of spring, so we do not have to wait much longer—only a month separates us from eternal cat bliss... Unfortunately, something is troubling me. My dear cat, you are not yet ready for our wedding. I must remind you that before we can get married, you must accomplish a feat. A feat in my honor!

Baguette answered immediately:

The Feat

My Breathtaking Cat,

The thought of our upcoming nuptials fills my heart with sheer joy. Believe me, I am ready for our wedding. Do not worry about the feat—it's done. You see, two winters ago I traveled from the past into the future, fought an army of chiming clocks, infiltrated into the Land of Good Girls and rescued Polina from that world of the past. So there's your feat. I will leave the catching of slow and clumsy street pigeons to Noir. I do not bother myself with such trivialities.

The next letter from Purriana was delivered by Bonehead after his morning walk.

My Darling Baguette,

That won't do. You did not rescue Polina for me: you did it for the Petrov family. As for catching pigeons, that's not what I am suggesting at all. Who needs our pigeons, with their bird flu, their lackluster feathers and their tough meat? No, no, I am expecting something greater from you, my knight in shining armor, because you are ginger—a pure ginger.

Baguette read the letter twice to himself and then a third time out loud to Bonehead.

"Why doesn't she like what you did for the Petrovs? They're great people!" exclaimed Bonehead.

"She wants the feat to be in her honor."

"But I thought you said the feat was a mere formality?"

"I did say that," admitted Baguette, "but my bride-to-be doesn't seem to agree. Evidently, she really does think of me as a knight...all because of my ginger coat...What's that got to do with it? Well, regardless, I'll do what she commands."

Baguette replied on a scrap of paper, in his decisive, masculine handwriting:

> *My heart belongs to you, O Wonderful Cat. What feat do you desire? Order me and I shall abide.*

"He's gone completely insane!" mumbled Bonehead as he carried the letter to Purriana. "'Order me and I shall abide?' I don't even say that to Papa Petrov, and he says it to some stray?!"

Purriana took the letter into her soft paws, quickly looked it over and scrawled a short response:

> *Meet me at midnight on the roof.*

CHAPTER 5

Disappearance

Polina sobbed, her head buried in Baguette's favorite pillow.

"He'll come back!" her older brother Vadik reassured her, although he himself was not hopeful—he had heard that runaway cats rarely returned home and instead got lost in the big, noisy city.

"We'll put up 'Lost Cat' signs," said Papa, "and someone will surely find him!" He, too, wasn't hopeful.

"I told you we should have put bars in the windows!" Mama scolded.

"Darling, he left through the door," retorted Papa. "What do you expect when all he hears is talk of bars?"

Bonehead lay sadly on his doormat. He knew better than anyone that Baguette had run away to be with Purriana. Bonehead did not approve of this decision, not one bit, but since the cat was his friend he had even helped him run away. Earlier that evening, when Bonehead and Papa returned from their walk, he had grabbed the grocery bag from Papa's hands and began running around the apartment, leaving a trail of yogurts, cheeses, cookies and cold cuts all over the floor. Papa dashed after Bonehead, forgetting to close the front door—and with the greatest of ease Baguette fled the apartment.

"I've already come up with what the sign will say," Vadik said. "'Lost Cat. Ginger, long-haired, pure-bred, prone to heroic acts. If found, please return to the Petrov family.'"

"No, no, that won't work," said Mama. "Think about it. Who would want to return a pure-bred, heroic cat to his original owners? Plus, you don't have anything about a reward. Without a reward, finders become keepers."

"What can we offer as a reward?" asked Polina.

"Something useful," said Mama, "but not too expensive."

"OK, we'll write this: 'Lost Cat. Ginger, mixed-breed, easily frightened. If found, please return to the Petrov family for a modest reward.'"

"I don't like that last part," said Papa. "'For a modest reward' seems discouraging. How about this: 'Reward: Papa Petrov's monthly salary'?"

"Darling, as always, you've got it!" said Mama. "Your salary is just right—after all, it's the perfect sum to buy nutritious yogurt for the whole family—ten whole cartons. But it's not too big. As for me, I'm ready to give my diamond ring for our cat. Of course, the diamond isn't real, but it's still very pretty. I'd be proud to show it off at a party."

"And I'll give away the medal I got for getting straight A's," said Vadik.

"And I'll give away my cactus," added Polina, "my very favorite cactus, which is always green, even in the winter."

In half an hour's time, Vadik had hung signs up all over the neighborhood:

LOST
GINGER CAT

> *He is meek and a mixed-breed, so he's not much use to anyone. If found, please return him to us, the Petrovs. As a reward you will get Papa's monthly salary, Mama's ring with an imitation diamond, a gold medal and an eternally green cactus.*

The signs hung on the sides of buildings, inside breezeways, on lamp-posts, on trees and at bus stops. The spring breeze fluttered them about, playing with the tear-away strips of telephone numbers. It ripped down some of the signs and carried them far, far away—to other streets, to other towns, and even to other countries.

CHAPTER 6

Rendezvous

The round yellow moon hung in the night sky like the surprised eye of a cat.

"Let's see what they're offering for you," dreamily purred Purriana.

She and Baguette had been rubbing noses and looking into each other's eyes when one of the signs fluttered over in the wind.

"'As a reward you will get...' Wow!" Purriana rubbed her eyes with her striped paw. "Money, diamonds, gold...The Petrovs must really love you!"

"And they respect me," proudly added Baguette. "Although..." Baguette carefully read the sign, "'He is meek and a mixed-breed'...Meek? Mixed-breed? Me, the cat who accomplished a heroic feat all for them?! No, they don't have an ounce of respect for me! Not a drop! Well, then, I won't be returning to them. I'll just go wherever the wind takes me."

"Well, it just so happens the wind is blowing in exactly the right direction. My great-great-grandmother lives in the attic of that neighboring building," said Purriana. "Let's go there."

"Why do I need to see your great-great-grandmother?" asked Baguette.

"She'll tell you about your feat...the one you must accomplish in order to marry me," Purriana responded modestly.

"The feat? Yes, of course, the feat...but still, why your great-great-grandmother? Why don't you tell me yourself? After all, this feat is to be in your honor!"

"Well..." For a second Purriana hesitated. "My great-great-grandmother knows more about these things."

"Why?"

"Because she knows everything. She's an oracle."

"A what?" Baguette was confused. "What kind of animal is an oracle? Or...or...ora...you're not saying she's a mouse, are you?" Baguette's fur stood on end.

"No," laughed Purriana. "She's not a mouse."

"That's good," sighed Baguette, "because, I've got, you know, an instinct. I catch mice—I can't help it. It's a good thing your great-great-grandmother isn't a mouse, but a...a..."

"An oracle," repeated Purriana.

"Yes, an oracle. Well, I hope that's still a member of the cat family."

"An oracle," explained Purriana, "is a type of prophet. She

can see the present, the past and the future. She's been waiting for you for quite some time."

"For me?" asked Baguette.

"Yes, for you," insisted Purriana, "because you're ginger."

"What does that have to do with it?"

"You'll see."

And so they set off for the neighboring roof.

CHAPTER 7

The Oracle

"Good evening, Great-great-grandmother. I've brought you the ginger cat named Baguette," said Purriana.

"Good evening," came a voice from the farthest corner of the attic. "Come closer, my children."

Baguette and Purriana came closer. The great-great-grandmother was curled up in a rocking chair. She was very old. Her fluffy, stripy, smoky-gray tail hung all the way down to the floor. Her graying whiskers, curled up at the edges as if in retro-fashion, were wispy from old age, and above her ears you could see white patches of skin where the fur was thinned out. Her striped fur had lost its luster but was well groomed and had the cozy appearance of a soft rug. Her eyes were closed.

"Even closer," she insisted. "I want to take a good look at the ginger cat."

"Maybe if she opened her eyes, she could see me better?" whispered Baguette, but still he came right up to the chair and, as a sign of respect for the elder cat, rubbed against one of its legs.

"No, she couldn't," whispered back Purriana. "Great-great-grandmother is blind."

"But…" began Baguette, but stopped as a soft paw slowly and carefully began to feel his nose, ears, back, tail and paws.

"Ginger!" elatedly exclaimed Great-great-grandmother after she had finished her inspection. "He is completely ginger, purely ginger, entirely ginger, undeniably ginger."

"How can you tell?" asked Baguette. "Not only are you blind, but your eyes are closed."

"I am an oracle," Great-great-grandmother said proudly. "I can see the present, the past and the future. I do not see with my eyes."

"What do you see with?" asked Baguette. "Your paws?"

"My young friend," explained the old cat, "like all oracles I see with my inner eye, not with my paws. The questions

you ask are rather ignorant. If I could not see that you are a ginger cat with the most honorable bloodline, I would think you were uneducated. But I can see that you are clearly pure-bred. Thus, I solemnly greet you, O worthy descendant of the ginger Catlanteans, and—"

"Ginger…cat…Who?" interrupted Baguette.

"Another ignorant question!" Great-great-grandmother exclaimed in frustration, flicking her tail.

"Excuse me, I must simply have misheard. Who am I the descendant of?"

"You are the descendant of the Catlanteans," graciously repeated Great-great-grandmother. "The ginger Cat-lan-teans," she said with emphasis.

Baguette felt like he was going to start molting from all his ignorance and embarrassment.

"And who are the Catlanteans?" he asked timidly.

For a few seconds, the oracle looked at Baguette in shock. Her gray tail swung from side to side like the pendulum of a clock. Finally she turned to Purriana.

"Does he really not know anything?!" she asked her. "What dumpster did you dig him out of?"

"He's a house cat, that's all," replied Purriana.

"Oh, that's all," Great-great-grandmother said with relief, her tail returning to stillness. "So, he's an orphan? He grew up without parents?"

"Yes, without parents," confirmed Baguette. "I was raised by humans, the Petrovs."

"The Petrovs...Hmm, the Petrovs," the oracle repeated, deep in thought. "Ah, the ones who live on the twelfth floor?"

"Yes, exactly."

"Yes, they are good people," the oracle pronounced after a short pause. "They do not hurt cats, they give them treats—a frankfurter, some chicken skin. They have a dog, too, a respectable fellow. He does sometimes chase Noir, but he treats all other cats with respect...Yes, they are good people, but people can never replace cats. Do you remember your father?"

"No," Baguette shook his head sadly.

"What about your mother?"

"Only a little bit. I remember that she was ginger and fluffy and always talked about France...I think her great-great-great-grandfather came to Moscow from France a long time ago. In a delivery truck with long loaves of bread."

For some reason this made the old cat laugh.

"Long loaves of bread!" she repeated.

"What's so funny about that?" asked Baguette.

"Nothing, my ginger friend," said the oracle, who had stopped laughing. "It's just you really do not know anything about your ancestors. But I will tell you about them now. Once upon a time, when apes had not yet turned into humans and wolves had not yet turned into dogs, there was an island in the middle of the ocean called..."

CHAPTER 8

The Legend, as Told by the Oracle

Once upon a time, when apes had not yet turned into humans and wolves had not yet turned into dogs, there was an island in the middle of the ocean called Catlantis. The inhabitants of this island were the beautiful and mighty Catlanteans—a race fathered by Pussiedon. One day the terrible god came down from the heavens to visit the island. As he was strolling through the fragrant flora of Catlantis, he happened upon a beautiful multicolored panther in the undergrowth. The panther was so frightened by the sight of the mighty Pussiedon that she ran away.

"O beautiful panther!" Pussiedon yelled after her. "Why are you running away?"

"It's you. You look so terrible and threatening—it makes my fur stand on end!" replied the panther from the undergrowth.

"Don't be afraid, I won't hurt you," said Pussiedon. "It's true, I am indeed terrible but your beauty has filled my heart with love. I like the four colors of your coat: white, like pure mountain snow; gray, like the sky before a thunderstorm; black, like the deepest ocean and ginger, just like a carrot."

"All right, I won't run away," agreed the panther. "O mighty god, what is it that you want?"

"I like your multicolored coat so much that I, a real immortal god, would like to take you as my wife, O simple mortal panther."

"Very well, then," said the panther and walked out from the undergrowth.

"We shall have the wedding immediately!" said Pussiedon. "And you'll birth me six kittens—but we can leave that until tomorrow. I will call them the Catlanteans. The first Catlantean will be white, like pure mountain snow. The second Catlantean will be gray, like the sky before a thunderstorm. The third will be black, like the deepest ocean. And the fourth will be ginger, just like a carrot."

"What about the fifth and sixth?" said the panther.

"Oh, yes, I forgot about my daughters," Pussiedon realized. "The fifth will be striped: you can pick whichever colors you like best. And the sixth will be spotted: I'll leave the spots up to you as well... And now come here, so we can finally get married!"

"Before we get married, I have one more question," said the panther.

"Yes?"

"Since you're immortal and I'm mortal, how will our Catlantean children turn out?"

"Hmm, I don't know. Let's get married, have children and then we'll see. I do hope they take after me..."

"No, that won't do, my dear," said the multicolored panther. "I need some sort of guarantee. I need to be certain of their fates."

"Fine," nodded Pussiedon. "I'll explain. Since you are mortal, our children won't be able to live forever. However, since I am an immortal god, one life will clearly not be enough for them. I will give each of them nine lives."

"And their children?"

"And their children, and their children's children. In fact, all the descendants of our Catlanteans will have nine lives— that is, as long as—"

"As long as eternity?" interrupted the panther.

"No, my dear, nothing lasts that long. They will have nine lives as long as..." Pussiedon looked around in search of something he could rely on. "As long as they inhale the aroma of these wonderful Catlantic flowers."

"All right," agreed the panther, "that works for me. After all, Catlantic flowers aren't going anywhere, are they? Which means that the Catlanteans and their descendants will always have nine lives!"

"So, we're getting married?" Pussiedon asked impatiently.

"Yes, dear."

And so they were married. The next day the multicolored panther gave birth to six kittlanteans. Four boys: one white, like fresh mountain snow; one gray, like the sky before a thunderstorm; one black, like the deepest ocean and one ginger, just like a carrot. And two girls: one with white, gray, black and ginger stripes, and one with white, gray, black and ginger spots.

Soon the kittlanteans grew into Catlanteans and gave birth to their own kittlanteans, who gave birth to more kittlanteans, and so on and so on. White, gray, black, ginger, striped and spotted Catlanteans populated Catlantis, and every Catlantean lived nine long and happy lives. The Catlanteans inherited wit and beauty from their ancestress, the multicolored panther, and magical abilities from the god Pussiedon. The Catlanteans could travel through time and space in a matter of seconds, they could see without using their eyes, they could hear without using their ears and they understood the fundamentals of both white and black magic.

On the island of Catlantis it was always summer, and the fragrant herbs and flowers grew year-round. The warm waters of the Catlantic Ocean lapped at its shores. Their turquoise waves brought fish, shrimp and oysters from the depths of the ocean and left them on the shore—gifts to the Catlanteans from the ocean gods. Three times a day, delicious birds would fall from the sky—leftovers from the sky gods' feasts. And by order of the earth gods, mice would voluntarily leave their burrows and wait patiently for the Catlanteans to catch them.

Day after day the Catlanteans swam, sang, wrote poetry and lounged in the sun. They ate the gifts of the ocean, sky and earth. They thanked the gods and brought up little kittlanteans. Everyone lived in peace and happiness—that is, until the cat-aclysms began. The island was struck by hurricanes and downpours, earthquakes and tornadoes, twisters and gales…and then came the cat-astrophe: the island began to sink. In only a few hours the beautiful Catlantis sank all the way to the bottom of the Catlantic Ocean!

Almost all the Catlanteans sank along with the island. Only a few survived—those who, at the very beginning of the cat-astrophe, scampered up trees and dug their claws into the bark. The storm winds ripped the trees from the ground and hurled them far into the ocean. The trees swayed on the waves and the surviving Catlanteans clung to them for dear life, watching from a safe distance as their wonderful, cherished island sank beneath the waters.

When the island finally disappeared, the Catlanteans all burst into tears.

"This is the end!" cried one.

"Our homeland is gone!" cried another.

"We'll drown!" lamented some.

"We'll be eaten by sharks!" sobbed others.

Only six Catlanteans remained calm. One was white, like fresh mountain snow, the second gray, like the sky before a thunderstorm, the third black, like the deepest ocean, the fourth ginger, like a carrot, the fifth striped and the sixth spotted. Silent and intent, they were looking at the horizon, each clutching a bunch of Catlantic flowers saved from their lost island.

"It seems we alone have kept a cool head at this

unprecedented hour," said the ginger Catlantean. "We're the only ones who thought to save the Catlantic flowers, the flowers whose fragrance gives us nine lives."

"Yes, yes," replied the white Catlantean. "Now we must preserve these flowers for all our brothers and sisters." He watched the trees as they floated by—frightened Catlanteans clung to them like wet leaves.

"Why would we do that?" said the black Catlantean. "If we share there will be less for us."

"No! We should take pity on them, they all need our help!" said the spotted one.

"She's right," agreed the striped one. "I can see it clearly with my third eye: if we do not want to disappear from the face of the earth, the surviving Catlanteans must help each other."

"And so we shall," declared the gray Catlantean. "We shall help all of them. We shall find our way to the mainland and replant our Catlantic flowers somewhere new and wonderful." Looking around, he added: "Preferably, somewhere far from water."

"We will become the wise rulers of a new country!" said the ginger one.

That is when the Catlanteans created the Council of Six—the famous Catlantic council, which to this day consists of the six wisest representatives of each Catlantic breed: white, gray, black, ginger, striped and spotted.

Soon enough, the surviving Catlanteans reached solid

ground. They inspected every corner of the world, planting a Catlantic flower in each one. They walked the earth six times over but never found a country as wonderful as the one they had lost. Resigned to their new life, the Catlanteans scattered about the world. They tried to keep away from large expanses of water, settling in woods, bogs and cities, making homes in basements and attics, colonizing dumpsters and human homes. In short, the mighty Catlanteans turned into the most ordinary of cats. Unlike their ancestors, who had loved splashing about in the ocean, they shuddered even at the tiniest spray of water. The memory of the great vortex that swallowed up their wonderful island remained forever in their hearts.

But the saddest thing of all was that the cats gradually began to lose the magical abilities they had inherited from Pussiedon. They forgot how to travel in time and space, how to see without using their eyes and to hear without using their ears and how to practice white and black magic.

That is when the wise Council of Six gathered atop Mount Aracat in faraway Catmandu. They waited until there was a full moon and prayed in desperation to their ancestor, Pussiedon.

"O Father!" yelled the members of the Council. "As you can see, we're now just ordinary cats! We barely resemble the wonderful Catlanteans. Yes, we still have the Catlantic flowers and we still have nine lives—but who needs all those lives when we've lost our homeland and are now losing our magical powers? Take pity on us, O powerful Pussiedon, take pity on your children! Please, leave us with something from the wonderful Catlanteans!"

And the mighty Pussiedon took pity on the cats. He left each breed with one magical ability.

Striped cats were left with the ability to see without using their eyes: that is, they could look into the past and foretell the future.

Spotted cats were left with the ability to hear without using their ears: that is, they could read people's minds.

Ginger cats were left with the ability to time travel: that is, they could travel between the past, the present and the future.

Gray cats were left with the ability to cross the frontiers of space: that is, they could travel from east to west to north to south in a mere instant.

White cats were left with the ability to practice white magic.

And black cats were left with the ability to practice black magic.

That night the Council of Six thanked Pussiedon. As the sun rose they left Mount Aracat—each one of them possessing a single magical power.

To this day, most, though not all, cats have one of these magical powers.

CHAPTER 9

The Prediction

The oracle finished her story and stretched gracefully in her rocking chair. Baguette and Purriana sat on the floor silently pressed up against each other.

"But why?" Baguette finally broke the silence. "What brought the cat-aclysms to Catlantis? What caused the cat-astrophe? Everything seemed so perfect…"

"That, I do not know," answered Great-great-grandmother. "The legend does not tell us."

"But you're an oracle," Baguette said with surprise. "You're a striped oracle who can see without using your eyes, you can look into the past and foretell the future. Why don't you look into the past, into the time of Catlantis, and answer my question: what caused the cat-astrophe?"

"That was too long ago," answered the oracle. "I cannot look that far into the past. But I am hoping that you, Baguette, will be able to."

"Me?" Baguette asked in shock.

"Yes, you. This is the very feat that you must accomplish in honor of your beloved. You must travel into the past, to the wonderful Catlantis."

"But why?"

"Because of the Catlantic flowers," answered the oracle, "whose fragrance gave the Catlanteans nine lives. As I told you, the Catlanteans took these flowers from Catlantis and planted one in each corner of the world. For many centuries, every cat in the world would make a pilgrimage to the sacred catnip gardens—where the Catlantic flowers grew—breathe in their fragrance and so acquire nine lives. But then, in the fourteenth century, cats forgot the way to the gardens and they forgot what the Catlantic flowers looked like."

"What do you mean, forgot?" Baguette asked doubtfully.

"I mean exactly that: forgot. You see, the flowers were put under a magical hex and ever since then all the cats of the world have searched for the catnip gardens to no avail. You must help all of us. Before you can marry Purriana you must accomplish this feat: you must travel into the past—to the island of Catlantis—where you must pick a Catlantic flower, or better yet a whole bunch, and bring it back to the present. Then every cat will once again have nine lives."

"This is all very lovely," said Baguette, "and I'm very happy for all the cats, I mean, I'm happy for them in advance, that they'll all have nine lives again. Only, maybe some other cat can bring this flower back from Catlantis? And in the meantime I'll quickly catch a mouse, present it to Purriana and we'll get married. Deal?"

"No, Baguette," the oracle shook her head. "No other cat can get the flower. Only you can—you who are ginger, truly ginger, nothing but ginger and the worthy descendant of your breed. All the cats of the world have been awaiting you for many years."

"All the cats of the world? Awaiting me?" Baguette fearfully pressed himself into the floor.

"Yes, you, Baguette. Back in the fourteenth century, when the way to the catnip gardens was forgotten, an old striped French oracle predicted that the flower would be found many centuries later by a ginger cat whose name begins with the letter 'B.' Her prediction was recorded in the Cat-echesis, the great Codex of the Catlanteans."

"The letter 'B'? That's it?" protested Baguette. "Why, there are plenty of names that start with 'B': Boris, Bobby, Boots—"

"There is one more prediction," interrupted Great-great-grandmother. "My prediction."

"Yours?"

"Yes," said Great-great-grandmother huffily, arching her back. "If you must know, I am a member of the Council of Six. I am an oracle. I can see without using my eyes. I'm privy to many secrets."

"And what secrets have you seen?"

"Recently, I saw that the cat who will bring back the

Catlantic flower is ginger. His name starts with the letter 'B' and ends in the letter 'E,' and he—"

"I know plenty of names like that," interrupted Baguette. "Babe, Boogie, Bernie—"

"And who lives on the twelfth floor—"

"Who knows how many cats live on the twelfth—"

"In the neighboring house—"

"There are any number—"

"And who has already once traveled in time, venturing into the past. So it is you—most definitely you."

And to this Baguette had absolutely no retort. It was definitely him.

"And since it is definitely you, I asked my great-great-granddaughter to inspire you."

"You asked her? You mean, it wasn't her idea? So, she doesn't love me? It's just because I'm ginger and you need some flower?" Baguette looked sadly at Purriana.

"Don't say such things, my darling," answered Purriana. "I won't lie, at first it was for that very reason. But now, after all the beautiful letters you've written me, after all the purrenades you've sung to me, after we've rubbed noses in the moonlight—now I've truly fallen in love with you. I really do want to marry you—but first you must accomplish this feat and bring my great-great-grandmother a Catlantic flower."

"Will it be dangerous?" timidly asked Baguette.

"Very dangerous," said Great-great-grandmother. "Catlantis

existed a very long time ago, a thousand years ago, or maybe even a million. You may not be able to reach it. You may drown in the depths of time. Or you may reach it and then drown in the depths of the Catlantic Ocean—the one that swallowed up the island..."

"Well...then maybe we can just forget about this flower? I mean, we've gotten by without the thing..." Baguette turned to Purriana. "Let's just get married. Sure, we'll only have one life—but at least it'll be a properly guaranteed one."

"No, dear, that won't work," said Purriana sadly. "Great-great-grandmother is very old and soon she'll pass away. She says it'll be in the middle of spring—and she knows these things better than anyone."

"My condolences to your great-great-grandmother, but I still think we should—"

"Don't interrupt me, ginger. It's rude," said Purriana. "Listen to me and you'll understand. My great-great-grandmother predicted that the ginger cat from the twelfth floor would bring back the Catlantic flower before she passed away. She told the Council of Six."

"So?" asked Baguette.

"One time, Great-great-grandmother made a wrong prediction. It only happened once but it was wrong all the same. As the striped member of the wise Council of Six she cannot afford to make another mistake. If she's ever wrong again, if the ginger cat from the twelfth floor—that is, you—doesn't bring back the flower by the middle of spring, it'll mean that the descendants of the striped Catlanteans have lost their ability to see into the future. And the entire breed of striped oracles will disappear from the face of the earth. So the wise Council of Six has determined."

"Disappear from the face of the earth? What do you mean?"

"I mean that soon, there'll be no more striped cats," explained Purriana. "I'll have to marry a black cat and all the striped cats of the world will have to do the same. We'll be the last striped cats in the world because when we mate with black cats we'll give birth to black kittens, since black is the most powerful color of all. Only you, Baguette," Purriana looked at him through tears, "only you can save the striped cats of the world from this terrible fate."

"To be honest," said Baguette in a quivering voice, "I don't really care about all the striped cats of the world. But you, O Wonderful Cat, I'm not letting any black cat have you. You'll be mine—even if I have to risk my life to accomplish the greatest and most heroic feat in all of feline history. And so," Baguette arched his back, "and so, I agree to set off for Catlantis to find the flower."

"Thank you, my love," whispered Purriana.

"Stay safe, courageous ginger Catlantean!" wished the oracle.

"Oh, Madame, you're too much." Baguette waved his paw. "I'm no Catlantean: I'm just an ordinary cat, an ordinary lovesick cat."

"I'll wait for you," said Purriana, rubbing her soft pink nose against Baguette's strong masculine nose.

"I'll be back," said Baguette, leaving the attic with dignity.

But there was something he failed to see: just outside the attic there was a cat with his ear pressed to the door. It was Noir.

CHAPTER 10

The Trash Man

No one—not Baguette, not Purriana, not even the oracle—noticed Noir at the door because he was as black as the deepest ocean, as black as coal, as black as night. None of them knew that Noir had heard their conversation.

After Baguette had left the attic, Noir quickly ran down the fire escape, silently jogged to his alley, jumped onto the dumpster and stared at the round yellow moon with his round yellow eyes.

"In the name of night darkness!" he yelled. "In the name of underground gloom and oceanic murk! I, black sorcerer and descendant of the black Catlanteans, order you to come forth! Come forth, O Trash Man! Rise up from the filthy dumpster, emerge from the trash—from candy wrappers and meat scraps, from potato and carrot peelings, from uneaten chicken bits and expired cans of fish! Come forth to serve and obey me! To follow my every order! Come forth immediately! Meowbra-catabra! Meowbra-catabra!"

At that moment, one of the dumpster lids opened to reveal the Trash Man. He was wearing a dirty brown trench coat, an old cap with a rusted gold star and military boots that went up to his knees. His eyes were invisible behind the blurred lenses of huge horn-rimmed glasses. The Trash Man climbed out of the dumpster and dusted himself off.

"I'm here, Boss," said the Trash Man in a hoarse, sickly voice. "I've come to follow your orders."

"Glad to see you," said Noir. "It's about time I got some help around here. Here's my first order: there's this local cat—he's ginger, goes by the name Baguette—now he's about to travel back in time to get a very important flower. Your job is to catch him as he's returning and steal the flower."

"And what if he comes back without the flower?"

"Well, then...then we'll play it by ear."

"Sounds good, Boss. It'll be done, Boss."

"Great. By the way, if you're hungry, feel free to help yourself," said Noir, motioning towards the dumpster.

"Thanks, Boss," said the Trash Man. He smiled, revealing yellow teeth. "Don't mind if I do."

And he proceeded to dig through the trash enthusiastically.

CHAPTER 11

The Eyes of Time

In order to travel from the present into the past, Baguette had to stop time. He had to put it to sleep. Make it stand still. He had to turn time into eternity.

Once time was asleep, the cat had to walk through it quietly—quietly and carefully, so as not to wake it. Because if time woke up, it wouldn't let the cat go—Baguette would be stuck between the past and the present, in the depths of time, all alone, forever.

Stopping time isn't easy: time runs very fast, so fast that you can't even see it. The only thing you can do is look into its alert, round eyes. We look into the eyes of time every day and they look back at us. Time has thousands of eyes—because the eyes of time are clocks. Wall clocks, wristwatches, grandfather clocks, any and all sorts of clocks.

If Baguette wanted to stop time so he could travel from the present into the past, his yellow cat eyes had to stare into the eyes of time for a very long time. And as he stared, he had to quietly purr a purraby about the place he wanted to go. At first, time would slow down, then it would begin to fall asleep, and finally it would stop altogether...Granted, of course, the cat did everything just right.

Baguette did everything just right. He climbed down from the attic into the yard, walked through a breezeway and ended up on a big city street. Baguette had never been there before but he could feel that the eyes of time were somewhere nearby. He quickly jogged two blocks and found himself in a square. And there it was, in the center of the square: a big gray clock tower. Baguette sat down across from the tower and stared intently at the clock. Then he began his purraby.

> *Twinkle, twinkle, little star,*
> *How I long to travel far.*
> *Hear me purr my purraby,*
> *As I look you in the eye.*
>
> *There's a time I want to go,*
> *Somewhere long, long, long ago.*
> *Go to sleep now, purr, purr, purr,*
> *Twinkle, twinkle, all ablur.*
>
> *I will travel to Catlantis*
> *To the island of cat bliss.*

Catlantis

Sleepy, dreamy, meow, meow, meow,
Au revoir, goodbye, ciao, ciao.

Twinkle, twinkle, little star,
Oh, Catlantis is so far...

The cat stared at the clock and sang, while the occasional night-time passerby would point his finger at him.

"What a strange cat!" he'd say. "Sitting in the middle of the square and ogling the clock! Not moving a muscle, only purring!"

Baguette continued to stare at the clock and sing. Soon the hands on the clock slowed down, and the hands on the watches of the people in the street slowed down, and the people themselves slowed down, and the cars slowed down and even the plane, blinking its red light up in the sky, slowed down. And then everything stopped: the hands on the clock, the hands on the watches, the people, the cars, the plane...

Baguette looked around. The cars were standing stock still at the intersection, even though the traffic light was burning green—welcoming them to go ahead. Two people were frozen in funny poses: one was pointing at him and the other was standing on one leg—his other leg was suspended in midair above a puddle the person was just about to step over. Baguette came a little closer to the people and saw that their eyes were closed. Then he looked up and saw that the airplane's red light had stopped blinking—it hung motionless in the night sky. The cat was sure that all the passengers in the airplane were fast asleep in their seats. The pilot, too, was asleep in the cockpit, and the copilot and the dogs and cats traveling in the baggage compartment in cages... Everyone was asleep. Because time had fallen asleep.

Only the ginger Baguette was awake. He knew that he had to hurry, because soon everyone would wake up. He took a final glance into the frozen eye of time and stealthily took off across the square in the direction of the past.

At first, Baguette walked effortlessly, just like always. But soon everything around him—the houses and the trees, the square, the big street and the sidewalk beneath him—everything began to quiver, to melt, to dissolve... That's when it became much harder to walk, as if the air had thickened and solidified, while the ground had turned into jelly.

And then, everything disappeared. Baguette couldn't see a thing. All he could sense was a cold, gray emptiness all around him, an emptiness that made it impossible to walk since his paws had nothing to grip. All of a sudden Baguette felt like he was drowning. He was slowly sinking to the bottom of some unknown body of water. Just then, it finally dawned on him—he was in the ocean. The Ocean of Time. *If I don't start swimming, I'll be stuck here forever!* thought Baguette. So he began to swim. He began paddling

energetically with all four paws, even helping with his tail. He continued swimming in the motionless ocean, going farther and farther into the past, until at last he saw a glimmer of light in the distance.

Baguette swam towards it. The light grew brighter and brighter, finally forming a blindingly bright orb. Baguette shut his eyes tightly, pressed his ears to his head and dived into it. The shining orb covered him in warmth, grabbed him and gently tossed him ashore...

CHAPTER 12

The Catlanteans

Baguette opened his eyes. He was lying on a warm golden beach, basking in the rays of the midday sun while lapping sapphire waves gently tickled his back paws.

Catlantis! thought Baguette and sniffed the air. It was filled with the honey-sweet fragrance of tropical herbs and flowers. Baguette got up, did some cat stretches—he arched his back, then rounded his back, arched, then rounded—and looked around. Fragrant flowers were everywhere—red, orange, periwinkle, blue, yellow, violet, white and pink, big and small, with thorns and without them, with small leaves that looked like lace and with huge leaves that looked like elephant's ears. Huge chocolate-colored butterflies and tiny colorful birds flew happily from flower to flower.

"The Catlantic flowers!" whispered Baguette. "Now all I have to do is to pick a bunch and . . ." Baguette started in the direction of the big red flowers, then turned towards the little yellow buds, then noticed a thorny stem crowned with a velvety blue flower, then decided to walk over to the pink flowers with golden centers, when finally he stopped in thought.

"Which ones do I want? Which of these flowers give cats nine lives?" He sat down in the sand, scrunching up his eyes in thought.

"Maybe my ancestral memory will help me out? I'll concentrate really hard and I'll remember. I'm sure that the flower will appear before my inner eye. I just have to concentrate really hard... Yes, I'll remember it, I'm sure I will..."

But the flower never appeared before his inner eye; instead, what appeared was a frankfurter. A big, pink frankfurter that the cat was dying to eat and also a fish head—a juicy trout head or maybe a salmon head... Baguette was very hungry.

Suddenly, something slippery plopped down on Baguette's tail. Shuddering, Baguette recoiled, then cautiously looked back. In the spot where he had been sitting lay a fish. A giant whole fish, freshly caught—well, freshly jumped—from the ocean. A moment later, a shrimp landed next to the fish. The next wave brought a handful of juicy open oysters. Baguette licked his lips and looked around. The beach was covered in generous gifts from the ocean gods: mussels, squid and octopus were toasting in the sun, huge crabs were feebly moving their pincers, fish of all types and sizes stared blankly from their giant eyes.

"Lunch! Lunch!" came a loud and beautiful voice from up above.

Baguette began to eat greedily but after only a few moments

he heard rustling coming from behind him. He turned around and his jaw dropped—the fish tail in his mouth fell to the ground.

Stretching sleepily, unimaginably magnificent creatures were coming out from the undergrowth. They were almost like cats, only twice as big as cats, twice as grandiose as cats, fluffier, stronger and more elegant than cats. Some were white, like fresh mountain snow; others were gray, like the sky before a thunderstorm; some were black, like the deepest part of the ocean; others were ginger, just like a carrot; others striped and still others spotted. Their coats shone in the sunlight and their eyes sparkled with a happiness that comes from not having a care in the world. Their tails were proudly lifted towards the heavens because they were not afraid of anything or anyone. They were the Catlanteans, the wonderful Catlanteans, the descendants of the god Pussiedon and the multicolored panther.

The Catlanteans came out from the undergrowth and began to eat. Baguette fearfully pressed himself into the sand.

"Look, what a precious little kittlantean!" A gray Catlantean pointed to Baguette.

"He's so little! But he's beautiful and ginger, just like me," said another Catlantean finishing off a shrimp.

"Such a baby and already he's trying to eat solid fish!" said a striped one.

"I'm not a baby!" said Baguette, offended. "Sure, I may be

smaller than you, but I'm an adult cat, a heroic cat who has come to you from the future..." His words were drowned out by the cheerful laughter of the Catlanteans.

"Of course you are!" laughed the Catlanteans. "You're our little hero! You came from the fu-fu-hahaha! Who's your mother? And where's your father?"

"I'm an orphan."

"There aren't any orphans on Catlantis! Don't be silly, little kittlantean, tell us who your parents are."

"I was raised by humans. The Petrovs."

"Humans?" The Catlanteans were surprised. "Who are humans? We've never heard of this animal, they don't live here on Catlantis."

"Humans walk on their hind legs. They don't have claws or tails or fangs; they don't even have fur, and in order to not get cold they have to wear the fur of other animals..." Baguette began to explain.

"Animals like that don't exist! That's too funny... You're quite the joker, our little ginger one!"

"I'm not little!" Baguette spat back. He quickly buried his fish scraps in the sand and jumped into the bushes.

It seems they aren't so wise after all, these Catlanteans! They don't even know basic facts! thought Baguette, watching the Catlanteans from the undergrowth.

Meanwhile, the Catlanteans finished their feast and a white Catlantean with prominent whiskers spoke to the crowd: "Brothers and sisters! As tradition dictates, let us give thanks to the gods of the ocean for this delicious and filling lunch!" With these words, he spread out his front paws, tucked his tail and bowed his head in front of the ocean. The other Catlanteans followed his lead—that is, everyone except a black Catlantean.

"Catlanteans!" cried out the black Catlantean to everyone's surprise. "To whom are you bowing down? In whose honor are you tucking your tails?"

"We're bowing down to the ocean gods. They feed us and we tuck our tails in their honor."

"Who else do you bow down to every day?" asked the black Catlantean.

"We also bow down to the gods of the sky and the gods of the earth," merrily answered the Catlanteans. "They give us food and we're thankful for it, so we tuck our tails in their honor."

"We're thankful," mocked the black Catlantean. "Wake up, brothers, wake up, sisters! We are the magnificent Catlanteans! Why should we thank anyone? Why should we grovel? Why should we bow and tuck our tails? We're only receiving that which is rightfully ours."

"You're wrong," protested the white Catlantean. "The food of the sky, ocean and earth does not belong to us. We receive it as gifts from the gods."

"From the gods? Where are they, these gods? Why don't they show themselves? Why don't they bring us these gifts themselves?"

"Yes, why not? Are they better than us?" A nervous energy began to spread among the Catlanteans.

"Hey, gods!" yelled the black Catlantean. "Where are you? Why don't you show yourselves? Maybe it's because you look down on us? Or maybe you don't even exist! Hey-o! Gods! Come out!" All the Catlanteans froze in anticipation, but nothing happened.

"You see," triumphantly continued the black Catlantean. "The gods don't exist. That is to say, we're gods. Fish jump out of the ocean for us of their own accord, birds voluntarily fall from the sky and mice decide to come out of their burrows. We're gods—the only gods! We don't need to thank anyone!"

"Yes, yes! We're gods!" the rest of the Catlanteans joined in. "The only gods! We don't need to thank anyone!" As the Catlanteans sang and danced they didn't notice that the blue sky had become gray, the sun had hidden behind a cloud and the smooth ocean waters had turned into frothy waves.

"Look, brothers and sisters!" cried the white Catlantean. "Look what's happening! The gods are angry with us! Stop dancing! Stop dancing immediately and bow down! Tuck your tails and beg the gods for forgiveness!"

"No way!" insisted the Catlanteans. "We're the only gods! We won't bow down or grovel ever again!" At that very moment a loud clap of thunder rang out. Baguette, still sitting in the bushes, decided to tuck his tail and bow down, just in case. An icy wind began to blow; thunder struck again, and with a silvery streak of lightning a downpour gushed from the sky.

"Brothers and sisters, look! Look how furious the sky gods are!" said the white Catlantean.

"Gods?" said the Catlanteans coolly. "It's raining and windy. So what? The weather just took a turn—that happens. What gods?" As soon as they said this, a gigantic murky wave came crashing onto the island's shore. As the wave rushed back to sea, the soaking, seaweed-covered Catlanteans looked at the frothing ocean in bewilderment.

"That's strange, I've never seen waves that big before," said the ginger Catlantean.

"It's the gods of the ocean—they're very angry with us!" insisted the white Catlantean. "Brothers! Sisters! Please, come to your senses and beg for forgiveness!"

"Never! We're the only gods. We refuse to tuck our magnificent tails ever again!" said the Catlanteans stubbornly.

So that's why the cat-aclysms began! That's what caused the cat-astrophe. The Catlanteans became haughty—they angered the gods, Baguette realized.

"We're the only gods!" cried the Catlanteans. "We're the only ones!" They began to dance again, but the earth began to tremble beneath their paws.

"The gods of the earth are angry too!" said the white Catlantean. "That's why the earth is trembling."

"It's just trembling because of our dancing!" laughed the Catlanteans. But in that instant a huge crack appeared on the earth's surface with a shattering rumble.

"Earthquake!" yelled the Catlanteans in shock, scattering in every direction. "Help us! Save us! We beg of you!" But it was too late for begging. Quaking and trembling, the magnificent Catlantis had begun to sink. The Catlanteans began to run amok in fear, Baguette along with them, but there was no safety in sight.

"You've angered us!" a deafening voice was suddenly heard coming from the ground, from the ocean and from the sky. "We're furious—you horrible, insolent cats! You don't deserve Catlantis. Scram! Shoo!"

The wonderful Catlantis was sinking. Distraught Catlanteans were jumping into the water or trying to dig their way into the ground for safety, but the smartest ones climbed to the tops of the trees. Baguette followed suit and scampered up a tall, thick oak.

"Hold on tight, little kittlantean," he heard someone say. Baguette turned around and saw a ginger Catlantean sitting on a nearby branch. One of his paws was tightly gripping the branch, the other was clutching a bouquet of white flowers.

"Are those the Catlantic flowers?" asked Baguette. "The ones that give nine lives?"

"The very ones."

"Grandfather," said Baguette (after all, the ginger

Catlantean was one of his forefathers, his great-great-great-great-great-great-great-great-and-so-on-grandfather, but to simplify, he just called him Grandfather). "Grandfather, may I please have a flower from your bouquet?"

"You're right, kittlantean," answered the ginger Catlantean. "You'll need this flower in that future of yours—the one with funny creatures who don't have claws and tails. Here!" And the ginger Catlantean held out a white Catlantic flower.

In that very moment, the earth quaked one last time and

the island submerged entirely under water. The place where Catlantis was only seconds ago was now just a giant vortex of water.

The murky ocean water took hold of Baguette and began spinning him towards the center of the vortex. Pitifully meowing and gripping the Catlantic flower with all his might, Baguette was streaming towards the black spinning eye of the vortex.

If I don't stop time, I won't make it back to the present—to my home, to the wonderful Petrovs and to my beloved Purriana! thought Baguette. *But how can I stop time? There aren't any clocks here! Poor me! Oh, poor, tragic, heroic me! I'll die in this horrible vortex, this spinning, eye-like vortex! Wait... Eye-like? Like an eye! Why, it's the eye of time!* Baguette realized happily. *It looks like a clock! And I, the ginger cat, I'm like the hands on a clock going around and around the eye.* And, continuing to spin, Baguette began his purraby.

> *Twinkle, twinkle, little star,*
> *How far I've come, how very far.*
> *Hear me purr my purraby,*
> *As I swirl around this eye.*
>
> *Poor Catlantis! Poor cat heaven!*
> *Poor Catlantis—drowned forever.*
> *Go to sleep now, sleepy time,*
> *As I purr this sleepy rhyme.*

Catlantis

I'm a ginger kitty cat,
Swimming in a vortex that
Swirls and swirls, round and round,
Help me, help me, not to drown.

Twinkle, twinkle, little star,
I have had to travel far…

As Baguette sang his purraby, the water in the vortex began spinning slower and slower and slower, until it fell asleep and stopped moving altogether. After he was sure that time had fallen asleep, Baguette stopped singing, grabbed the Catlantic flower in his teeth and began to swim, paddling with all four of his paws and even helping with his tail.

He swam and swam through the thick dark Ocean of Time; he swam, clutching the flower with his teeth; he swam, not knowing where he was going. In his haste to sing a purraby, he had forgotten to mention his destination.

Nonetheless, he really hoped that he would swim out of the ocean and end up in exactly the city square where he had started, not far from home. So when he saw a light ahead of him, he bravely swam right into the shining orb. The shining orb covered him in warmth, grabbed him and gently tossed him into the square…

CHAPTER 13

Panna Catta

Unfortunately, it was a different square. Instead of asphalt there was cobblestone, and instead of cars there were carriages being pulled across the square by whinnying horses. Sitting behind each horse was a person with a switch. He'd use it from time to time to whip the horse and sometimes even people dressed in rags—those who hadn't been paying attention and hadn't stepped out of the way. In the dis-tance, instead of familiar multistory buildings, Baguette saw a castle that was surrounded by a gray stone wall perched menacingly on a nearby hill. Instead of the big city street, Baguette saw a winding dirt road leading

down the hill from the castle. The road was bumpy and muddy. And instead of the usual shops with signs like "Flowers," "Tobacco" or "Ice Cream," there was a row of carriages and wooden stalls. They were filled with all sorts of barrels, kettles and pots, baskets with fruits and vegetables, trays of herbs and wooden slabs with hogs' heads staring blankly at Baguette. Street vendors dressed in aprons and caps were walking around the stalls, periodically yelling something in an unknown language. Actually, after listening carefully, Baguette realized the language wasn't so strange after all—it was French, his mother's native tongue.

Behind the row of stalls was a single lonesome flower stand. Wilted bouquets of violets and roses were draped across the florist's lap and a few trampled tulips lay on the ground beside her. She was dozing peacefully and since she wasn't yelling, no one was buying her goods. Only a slim, spotted cat was sniffing around her flowers.

When he saw the flowers, Baguette was reminded of the Catlantic flower. He looked down at the cobblestone street—the white flower was lying beside him, whole and unharmed. Yet, there was something strange about it. Upon closer inspection Baguette realized that the flower had become somewhat transparent. Looking through one of the petals, he could easily see the gray cobblestones and even a lost horseshoe nail. In fact, he could see the nail more and more—it was as if the flower were melting before his very eyes. Baguette lifted the transparent flower and looked through it at the various stalls, at the castle wall, at an ash-gray cloud . . .

"Don't disappear!" he whispered to the flower.

But the flower nodded its barely visible head in farewell, or perhaps simply drooped, and dissolved into thin air, leaving behind only a soft, pleasant aroma. A second later the aroma had disappeared as well.

"Shoo! Out of here!" Someone roughly kicked Baguette.

"Outta the way!" A whip cracked in the air, painfully catching Baguette's ear.

"Scram, you ginger stray!" one of the vendors scolded, throwing a cabbage core his way.

Pressing his ears to his head, Baguette jumped out of the way in fright.

"Come with me," he heard a voice say from behind. Baguette turned around and saw the spotted cat who had been sniffing at the flower stall.

"Come on! They don't like stray cats here!" The spotted cat led Baguette away from the square, into the twisting, smelly side streets of the unfamiliar town. Avoiding people's feet and horses' hooves, they zigzagged between small stone houses with red tiled roofs, heading towards a destination unknown to Baguette. Finally, they made their way out of the labyrinth of streets and found themselves in front of the hill on which the castle was perched. Motioning for Baguette to follow her, the cat began to climb the hill. Baguette obeyed. When they reached the stone wall surrounding the castle, the spotted cat pressed herself flat against the ground and quickly crawled through a thin crack underneath its heavy metal gate. Baguette did the same and found himself in a quiet and beautiful park. Carefully trimmed rose bushes grew alongside the park's paths. Past the bushes, on the shores of a sparkling pond, stood the castle. Birds were chirping happily in the treetops.

"You're safe here," said the spotted cat.

"Thank you," said Baguette politely. "But who are you? I didn't have a chance to ask you back in the square."

"My name is Panna Catta Catricia Catilda de Purr de Purrie Claire de—"

"Holy claw!" interrupted Baguette. "What a name! What were your parents thinking?"

"They were thinking of my great future. My father is the Cat King of France and my mother the Cat Queen of Italy... Well, *was* the Queen, until she was given to the French Duke."

"So now she's the wife of the Duke?"

"Who?"

"Your mother."

"How dare you! My mother is the wife of my father, the Cat King."

"Wait. I've gotten a little lost in your family tree," said Baguette smiling—he didn't really believe any of it. "You said your mother was given to the French Duke."

"Yes, the human French Duke. He lives in this very castle," she said, pointing to the castle, whose tower poked out above the treetops. "My father is the Cat King of France, a pure-bred gray cat—he's the Duke's favorite. When the Duke received my mother as a gift, he blessed her marriage to my father and I was born. I am the Princess Panna Catta Catricia Catilda de Purr de Purrie Claire de—"

"Princess?" asked Baguette quizzically. He emphatically looked her over, noticing her elegant but dirty paws and muddy coat. "But would the Princess, the lovely Panna Catta Catilda de whatchamacallit ..."

"You may call me Panna Catta."

"Would the lovely Princess Panna Catta allow herself to look like that?" finished Baguette.

"If she wanted to look a certain way, then yes, she would allow it." Offended, Panna Catta let out her claws—to Baguette's surprise they were quite clean and well manicured.

"So, you're a princess but you want to look like a stray?" asked Baguette, looking uneasily at her claws.

"Not always," replied Panna Catta, retracting her claws. "Sometimes I get bored sitting in the castle and playing with my Bolognese puppy companion. So I get myself dirty on purpose and go into town incognito."

"Incog... What's so neat-o?"

"In-cog-ni-to," repeated Panna Catta. "It means 'in secret'— so that no one in town will know I'm really a princess. Because if the stray cats see a princess they start bowing and flattering me and warning me about possible dangers... How boring! Incognito is better."

"I get it," said Baguette. Then he hastily added, "Your Highness."

"See! You're doing it too! Let's do away with the formalities, OK?"

"OK," agreed Baguette. He looked hopelessly at a rose bush growing near the wall and thought about the Catlantic flower—the one he brought all the way from Catlantis, the one that had dissolved into thin air. Like fog. Like a dream.

"Don't be sad. You can't bring back the Catlantic flower," the spotted Panna Catta consoled him.

"Yes, it disappeared, just like a dream... Wait a minute! How do you know about the flower?"

"I heard."

"You heard what?"

"You."

"But I didn't say anything!"

"I heard your thoughts. I have white, gray, black and ginger spots—I'm a spotted cat. Spotted cats can hear without using their ears."

"And what did you hear?"

"Well... You're a ginger cat..."

"That's obvious, you can see that!"

"Hush! I need to concentrate," Panna Catta shushed him in annoyance. "So... because you're a purely ginger cat you were sent back in time to Catlantis to get the Catlantic flower that gives cats nine lives. You got the flower but then it disappeared. Also, you're lost. You don't know where you are or what century you're in."

"Exactly. You're exactly right... I don't know where I am, what century I'm in or why the flower disappeared."

Panna Catta licked her paw and began cleaning herself. "I can help you with that."

CHAPTER 14

The Loyal Cat

"OK, let me explain," said Panna Catta. "You're in France. It's the Middle Ages—the fourteenth century to be exact. And the flower disappeared because you can't bring anything back from the past. Something that belongs in one time cannot live in another."

"How do you know that?"

"Everyone knows that. It's written in the Cat-echesis—the great Catlantic Codex—on the very last page. You can't take anything out of the past."

"But if it's written in the Cat-echesis, why did the striped oracle send me to Catlantis to get the flower?"

"How should I know?" huffed Panna Catta. "Although, wait. I think I understand what's happened. The last page of the great Catlantic Codex was ripped out only a few days ago. We all remember what it said, but all of you—living seven centuries in the future—of course you've all forgotten!"

"Who ripped the page out and why?"

"A criminal. A bad cat," said Panna Catta vaguely.

"Hey," Baguette looked at Panna Catta with hope, "in your so-called Middle Ages, do you have Catlantic flowers? I mean, do you still remember what they look like and where they grow?"

"Of course we remember," nodded Panna Catta. "And of course we have them. But you won't be able to take them from here into the future, just like you couldn't take them from Catlantis."

"Oh, we'll see about that. Can you take me to the flowers?"

"I don't need to take you anywhere. There's a catnip garden right here, inside the Duke's park."

"What are we waiting for? Let's go!"

"No, I'll pick a flower and bring it to you. You wait here. I can't take you any closer to the castle—if my Bolognese puppy companion sees you, she'll tell my father. And I'm not allowed to bring stray cats to the castle."

"I'm not a stray! I'm a free house cat..." But Panna Catta had already disappeared behind the trees. Soon Panna Catta returned with the flower in her teeth. Baguette took the flower—it was as white and as aromatic as the flower from Catlantis.

"Thank you," said Baguette, smelling the flower. "Hey, since I smelled the flower, I'll have nine lives! Right?"

"Well, if you stay here in the Middle Ages..." Panna Catta looked at Baguette flirtatiously. "Then yes, you'll have nine lives."

"And if I don't stay? If I return home?"

"Then, having nine lives isn't in your future. After all, you smelled the flower here, in the past. The flower's magic won't be effective in your time. And the flower will disappear again...I already told you that."

"We'll see if it disappears or not!" Baguette insisted stubbornly.

"Maybe you should stay," said Panna Catta sweetly. "Do you want me to take you to the castle and introduce you to my father? I can tell him that you aren't a stray but a foreign cat prince."

"Why?"

"I like you," said Panna Catta timidly. "In fact, I like you so much, dear ginger cat, that I, the Princess Panna Catta Catricia Catilda de Purr de Purrie Claire de...anyway, you get the idea...I want to marry you. We'll live nine long, happy lives together in this wonderful castle. We'll sniff the Catlantic flowers, eat fried quail, listen to the violin, play tag with my Bolognese puppy companion..."

"No," quietly said Baguette.

"No?"

"No," repeated Baguette, this time with conviction. "You're a very beautiful spotted cat, but I can't stay here with you. I have to return home."

"You're refusing me?!" Panna Catta's green eyes flashed with rage, she let out her claws and arched her back. "Me? The Princess Panna Catta Catricia Catilda de Purr de Purrie

Claire de … Anyway … Me, the spotted Panna Catta? Don't you know that if I say the word a pack of rabid dogs will be released to attack you? How dare you! You … Wait, what are you saying?"

"I'm not saying anything."

"Yes, you aren't saying anything but your thoughts are racing." Panna Catta retracted her claws, sat down in the grass and squinted. "Yes, yes … I understand … Why didn't you tell me you had a fiancée? What's her name? Oh, what a beautiful name, although it's quite short …" Baguette silently watched Panna Catta. Finally she opened her eyes and looked sadly at Baguette.

"Your thoughts told me that you have a fiancée whose name is Purriana and that you love her very much. You're staying loyal to her."

"It's true," said Baguette, preparing for the worst.

"Well, if that's the case, then I'll let you go. Love is a respectable explanation."

"Farewell, spotted Panna Catta, and thank you for the flower. I'm going back to the square—I saw a big clock there—I'll lull time to sleep and—"

"Not now!" interrupted Panna Catta. "Please, don't stop time right now. It's almost nightfall and tonight, exactly at midnight, there's to be a trial in the square. Time has to be running as usual. Please wait until the trial is over, then you can do whatever you want. Promise me you'll wait."

"I promise. But why is this trial so important to you?"

"Because the Council of Six is presiding over the trial. My father, the Cat King of France and a pure-bred gray, is not only a member of the Council but also a witness for the prosecution. I don't want your purraby to stop my father in mid sentence. This trial is very important to all of us."

"All right, all right, I'll wait until the trial is over. Who's being charged?"

"A witch," answered Panna Catta. "And her cat."

CHAPTER 15

The Trial

A full moon hung high above the square. It was yellow and very round, like the eye of a frightened cat.

Meanwhile, on the square itself a crowd was awaiting the trial. There was just one human being; the rest of the crowd was cats, Baguette among them. The cats had settled in comfortably, sitting and lying on the abandoned wooden stalls—those that earlier in the day had been packed with wares of every kind. The human, a man of medium height in a gray coat, was standing off to the side with a notebook in his hand.

In the center of the square, right below the clock, sat the two defendants: a raven-haired woman with hazel eyes who was wearing a bright red dress, and a big black cat. Across from them towered an empty wooden platform. Everyone was silent.

"Please rise. Court is now in session, the honorable Council of Six presiding," a loud voice boomed across the square.

Stretching to their full height the cats all stood up in their wooden stalls. Only the black cat, the defendant, remained seated at the feet of the raven-haired woman.

"Rise, Black Tony! Rise!" yelled the cat crowd.

"Not a chance," said the black cat calmly.

"Disrespecting the Council!" meowed a striped cat.

"Yes, disrespecting the Council!" echoed the other cats.

Disrespecting the Council, the man in the gray coat neatly wrote in his notebook.

"Here they come. Here comes the Council of Six. Tuck your tails in honor of the wise Council of Six," boomed the same voice. Five cats proudly walked onto the platform: one white, one gray, one ginger, one spotted and one striped.

"That's the Council of Six?" said Baguette.

"Yes," said a whitish-ginger cat be-side him.

"But why are there only five of them?"

"You really don't know?" said the cat in surprise. "The sixth member of the Council is the defendant—his name is Black Tony. There he is, sitting next to the witch."

"That young raven-haired woman is a witch?"

"Actually, she's one hundred and one years

old. She just looks really good for her age," said the cat. "Now shh! They're about to read the charges."

"And so," loudly began the eldest member of the Council of Six, the white cat, "the defendant, Black Tony, former member of the wise Council of Six, is being tried on six charges. The first charge: inciting revolution. The second charge: attempting to seize absolute power. The third charge: conspiring with a human—from which follow the last three charges. The fourth charge: breaking our Catolic vow of silence—you revealed mystical feline secrets to a human. The fifth charge: damaging Catolic property—you ripped the last page out of the Cat-echesis, the great Codex of the Catlanteans, and gave it to a human. And finally, the sixth charge: theft of the Catlantic flower—which you also gave to a human."

"I plead not guilty!" yelled Black Tony.

"To which charges?"

"To all of them."

The white cat frowned. "All right, then, we will go through the charges one by one. I must warn you, everything you say can and will be used against you. The first charge: inciting revolution. Black Tony, you tried to convince the Council of Six that six rulers is too many. You are quoted as having said, 'One is enough. Then there will be no disagreements or arguments.' Did you say these things?"

"I did," said Black Tony, "and the Council agreed with me. You all agreed that one ruler is better than six."

"Irrelevant," said the members of the Council in unison.

"The second charge," the white cat continued unfazed. "Attempting to seize absolute power. You tried to convince the Council to vote for you as the sole leader. Is this true?"

"Yes," said Black Tony, "and you all did the same. Each of you tried to convince the others to vote for you as the sole leader."

"Irrelevant," said the members of the Council in unison.

"The third charge: consorting with a human. Black Tony, after you failed to be elected as the sole leader—since every member of the wise Council of Six wisely voted for himself—you asked a woman for help. This woman"—the white cat pointed his paw at the raven-haired woman—"is a witch!"

"Objection!" said the woman. "I am not a witch."

"She's not a witch," said Black Tony. "Witches are old, ugly and have warts on their noses—while she's young and beautiful."

"Objection overruled," said the white cat. "According to our sources this woman is one hundred and one years old. Only witchcraft could make her so young and beautiful."

"This is unjustified! This is slander—I'm not a witch!"

"If you are not a witch, then how can you understand cat language?"

"I...I..." The woman was at a loss for words.

"She just has a knack for languages!" said Black Tony.

"You two are in cahoots, that's why you're defending her—you're a witch's familiar!" said the white cat. "No ordinary humans can learn our language—only witches!"

Understands cat language, noted the man wearing the gray coat. *Is in cahoots with the black cat.*

"Moving on, the fourth, fifth and sixth charges," continued the white cat. "Black Tony, you revealed mystical feline secrets to this witch. You told her about the great Catlantic Codex and about the Catlantic flowers. Then you gave her the last page of the Codex as well as a Catlantic flower. With these, she intends to brew a potion that will give the two of you unlimited power."

Brewed a potion out of flowers and pages from a holy book, noted the man wearing the gray coat.

"I plead not guilty! This is slander!" said Black Tony.

"I call the first witness to the stand," announced the white cat. The gray member of the Council of Six stretched his hind legs and proudly walked forward.

"Witness, please state your name and titles."

"I am the Cat King of France, a member of the Council of Six, a pure-bred gray. My name is Entrecât."

Ah! Panna Catta's father! thought Baguette.

The white cat placed a book in front of the gray cat.

"Your Majesty, Sir Entrecât. Do you swear by the Great Catlantic Codex that the evidence you shall give is the truth, the whole truth and nothing but the truth?"

"I do solemnly swear," answered Entrecât, with his paw on the Codex.

"Your Majesty, Sir Entrecât, in the name of Catolicism, please answer the Council's questions. Did Black Tony reveal the mystical feline secrets to this witch? Did he rip out the last page of the Catlantic Codex and give it to her? Did he give her a Catlantic flower from the catnip gardens?"

"Yes," nodded the gray cat, "yes and yes."

"How do you know this, Your Majesty?"

"I saw and heard it."

"When?"

"Last night."

"Lies!" screamed the defendant. "You gray liar! Last night you were in your castle hosting a ball. Everyone knows that!" The black cat turned to the crowd for support. The cats began whispering anxiously.

"It's true," conceded Entrecât. "Last night I hosted a ball. But, since I am a pure-bred gray cat, I am able to cross the frontiers of space in seconds: that is to say, I can be in two places at once. Last night I was at the ball and at the same time I peeked into the witch's den."

"There are no further questions," said the white cat. "The

Council has heard everything it needs to. It has reached a verdict. Woman with the raven hair, please stand. The Council of Six finds you guilty of witchcraft and pronounces you a witch. Since it is beneath our jurisdiction to try humans, we are turning you over to the human courts of the Holy Inquisition." The white cat turned to the man in the gray coat. "Take her away!" he ordered.

The man in the gray coat tucked his notebook into one of his pockets and produced a pair of handcuffs from the other one. He walked up to the woman and handcuffed her.

"In the name of the Holy Inquisition," he said in a flat monotone, "you, witch, are arrested." He led her away from the square, looking back at the Council and repeating, "Always a pleasure to work with you! It has been a pleasure, my dear animals!"

"You're the animal," the white cat said quietly. "Let us continue with the verdict. Black Tony, former member of the Council of Six, please stand. The Council finds you guilty on all six charges. You will be replaced in the Council by a newly elected black cat. You are sentenced to death. This is your eighth life so you still have one left—your ninth. As you can see, we are merciful. In addition, the Council of Six has ruled that from now on all black cats shall lose the right to smell the Catlantic flowers that give nine lives. From now on, every black cat will live only one life. That is the punishment for abusing black magic."

"Oh, so it's like that, is it?" said Black Tony. "You're forbidding my entire breed the right to smell the Catlantic flowers? Then you've brought this upon yourselves!" His eyes gleamed menacingly and he shouted, "In the name of night darkness! In the name of underground gloom and oceanic murk! I command all cats to forget what the Catlantic flowers look like and where they grow. From now on no cat will ever live nine lives! Meowbra-catabra! Meowbra-catabra!"

Upon hearing the terrifying curse the cats in the crowd began to howl in panic.

"What do the Catlantic flowers look like?" one cat whimpered. "I don't know! I've forgotten! Excuse me, do you remember what color they are? Blue? Red? Yellow? Are they big? Are they small?"

"I don't remember!" said a cat to her left.

"Me neither!" said a cat to her right.

"Do you know where they grow?"

"We don't remember!" the cats yelled.

"Ay, ay, ay! Our memory! What's happening to our memory?"

The Council members let out their sharp claws and their fur stood on end.

"What have you done, you filthy animal?" they cried. "You've taken away the knowledge we cherish most of all!"

"Glad to hear it," said Black Tony. "You've brought this upon yourselves. Now I alone will rule over these wonderful red... wait, no, blue... I mean, pink... holy claw! I've forgotten too!"

Yes, Black Tony had forgotten too. As he uttered his terrible curse, he had mistakenly said, "I command *all* cats to forget..."

*S*o that's how all the cats forgot what the Catlantic flowers look like and where they grow! thought Baguette. The Council of

Six condemned the black cat and in his wrath he put a curse on the flowers. Baguette got up, did some cat stretches—he arched his back, then rounded his back, arched, then rounded—and looked around. The square had almost emptied; the last few cats were leaving the site of the trial.

I guess it's time for me to go home. I just have to grab my Catlantic flower, the one I hid in a safe spot...Hmm, where was that again? In that moment Baguette realized he had completely forgotten where he'd hidden the flower. And what it looked like.

"Oh, no! Me too!" exclaimed Baguette. "Ah, the poor, heroic, ginger cat! My beloved Purriana and her great-great-grandmother are waiting for me at home. They're hoping I'll bring back the flower, but I'm returning empty-handed!" Baguette sat down in front of the street clock and woefully began his purraby.

> *Twinkle, twinkle, little star,*
> *I'm returning from afar.*
> *Hear me purr my purraby,*
> *As the tears pour from my eyes.*
>
> *I can't believe the time has come,*
> *The time has come to swim back home.*
> *The cats at home, everyone*
> *Will call out in unison:*

The Trial

"The flower! The flower! Where's the flower?
We want to smell its magic power!"
"Here I am, back from Catlantis,
But purrdon…I'm empty-handed."

Twinkle, twinkle, little star,
Oh, my home is very far…

The cat looked at the clock and sang his purraby. The clock's
hands began spinning slower and slower and slower and
slower, until they stopped completely.

CHAPTER 16

The Oracle's Mistake

The Petrov family had almost lost hope. The signs Vadik had hung up had yellowed and withered away and still no one called. The tear-away strips of telephone numbers fluttered in the spring breeze. Sometimes a gust would come from around the corner, rip down one of the signs and carry it far, far away, to other towns and even to other countries. The wind would carry the signs to St. Petersburg and Novosibirsk, to Samara and Bishkek, to India and Egypt, to Belarus and Thailand, to Spain and France. In place of the missing signs Vadik would diligently hang up new ones. But there were still no calls.

"Where's our cat?" lamented Papa Petrov. "Where could he have gone?"

"Haven't people seen the signs?" said Vadik. "I must've hung up at least a hundred thousand!"

"It's unbelievable, really," said Mama. "We're offering a lot for this cat—a month's salary, a ring with an imitation diamond, a gold medal and an eternally green cactus—and still no one has returned him to us."

"It can mean only one thing: no one has found him yet," said Papa.

"What if he got run over by a car?" cried Polina.

"What if he fell into a manhole?" said Vadik, turning pale.

"What if someone mean found him?" said Mama.

"What if he died of hunger?" said the grandfathers.

"What if he got sick?" said the grandmothers.

"What if a pack of dogs ate him?" whined Bonehead. "Some stray pit bulls or maybe bull terriers…"

T he Petrovs weren't the only ones who missed Baguette. Two cats were also waiting for him—his beloved Purriana and Purriana's great-great-grandmother, the striped oracle. In fact, the oracle was most impatient for Baguette to return. She was the one who had predicted that Baguette would return with the Catlantic flower before she passed away, which she knew was going to happen in the middle of spring—and the middle of spring it was.

The bright spring sunshine poured into the attic; it seeped through every crack and coated the darkest, dustiest, coldest spots that winter had left behind with its warmth. The striped oracle lay in her rocking chair, warming herself in the sun's rays. Her eyes were closed, her tail hung motionless, but she was not sleeping. She was deep in thought about the ginger cat. She knew her fate: she was going to pass away tonight at sunset—she hoped that the ginger cat would return before then. The ginger cat with the white flower.

Baguette was the oracle's very last chance. The future of all the striped cats depended on him. Because one time the oracle had made a wrong prediction. It only happened once, but it was wrong all the same. And oracles cannot be wrong twice. After her mistake, the wise Council of Six determined that if she were ever wrong again—if the ginger cat did not bring back the flower by the middle of spring—it would mean that the descendants of the striped Catlanteans had lost their ability to see into the future. Which would mean that the entire breed of striped cats must disappear from the face of the earth. All the striped cats would marry black cats and give birth to black kittens. And there would be no more striped cats. Ever.

"Maybe you'd like some milk?" said Purriana. She had been taking care of the oracle for the past few days. "Please, Great-great-grandmother, you aren't eating or drinking! You need strength—you have to be here when Baguette returns!"

"No, I don't want any milk," said the oracle, barely audibly. "I have all the strength I need to make it to sunset, and after that I won't need strength anymore—I'll be gone."

"Don't say that! Be careful what you wish for!"

"Striped cats don't wish: they predict."

"Well, then, don't predict! Why do you have to die at sunset? Why don't you predict something else?"

"That's not in my powers, Great-great-granddaughter. I know what is in store for me—tonight's sunset will be my last. I'm cold…" She shivered and wrapped her tail around her body. "Where is he? Where's your ginger fiancé?"

"Don't worry, Great-great-grandmother," said Purriana as she rubbed against the rocking chair. "He'll be here. He'll definitely be here. I'm sure that Baguette will bring the flower before sunset. Just like you predicted."

"I hope so. I truly hope so. I was wrong once before—I hope I'm not wrong again!" Purriana looked at her great-great-grandmother thoughtfully. "Great-great-grandmother, you've spoken so much about your wrong prediction," said Purriana timidly, "but you never told me what it was."

"It's a very unfortunate memory, Purriana. It was such a stupid mistake."

"But maybe…" Purriana rubbed against the chair once more, as a sign of utmost respect, "maybe you can tell me today? What was your wrong prediction?"

"All right," said the oracle, "I suppose I can tell you today. About a year ago, I had a vision…Or, rather, I thought I had a vision. The vision told me where to find the Catlantic flower. I called a meeting of the wise Council of Six and said, 'I, the striped oracle, saw without the use of my eyes where to find the flower that gives cats nine lives. A shipment of various plants was delivered to the neighborhood florist today and one of them is the Catlantic flower. It grows in a flow-erpot—the third pot on the second shelf to the right of the entrance. It is for sale and it costs mere pennies.' The wise Council of Six asked me, 'Oracle, what does the flower look like?' I told them I didn't know—I couldn't see the flower. But I could clearly see where it was in the shop. Someone was sent to the florist immediately to get the plant from the spot I had described. When they brought it back..." At this point the oracle sadly furrowed her brow. "When they brought it back, the plant was a...cactus."

"A cactus?"

"Yes, a cactus. An ordinary cactus that had nothing in common with a flower. That was my wrong prediction. The one that shamed our entire breed of striped cats."

"What happened to the cactus?" said Purriana.

"It was thrown away. It was taken to the alley and left near the dumpster. Noir circled the pot day after day in hopes of catching a whiff of the mag-ical Catlantic aroma but only ended up with needles in his nose. Soon after, some humans took it away. Actually, it was the Petrovs—Polina convinced her father to take it home. Apparently they still have the cactus. Polina keeps it on her windowsill."

"Oh, I see." Purriana nodded. "On her windowsill... Wait a minute! On her windowsill? So it's that very cactus? Holy claw!" Purriana dashed from the attic. "Holy moly claw!"

"Great-great-granddaughter," yelled the oracle after her. "What's a 'holy claw'? And where are you going?"

"We need that cactus!" shouted Purriana from the stairs. "Great-great-grandmother, your prediction wasn't wrong!"

"What do you mean, it wasn't wrong?" But Purriana was already on her way to the Petrovs' and didn't hear the oracle's question.

B ut someone else did—the Trash Man. He had heard their entire conversation. He was crouched down on all fours pretending to be a pile of trash near the attic door. His boss had ordered him to listen in on the two cats and report anything of interest back to him—to Noir.

CHAPTER 17

Monsieur de Tutu

Monsieur Jacques Saussure de Tutu was piping pastry cream into a batch of croissants when a crumpled piece of paper flew into his bakery through the open window. Monsieur de Tutu moved the croissants aside and flattened out the paper.

"*Oh, mon Dieu!*" said Jacques. "It's some sort of document—perhaps a very important one—but it's written in a foreign language!"

With these words, he hung a sign on his bakery door that said "back soon," closed it with a big padlock and went to see his friend Simoux Lacroum—a translator who knew every language and was very smart.

"Interesting, very interesting indeed," said Simoux Lacroum after reading the document. "Where did it come from?"

"The wind blew it into my bakery. What does it say?"

"It's a sign for a lost cat. It says: 'Lost Ginger Cat. He is meek and a mixed-breed, so he's not much use to anyone. If found, please return him to us, the Petrovs. As a reward you will get Papa's monthly salary, Mama's ring with an imitation diamond, a gold medal and an eternally green cactus.'"

"A ginger cat..." repeated Jacques. "A ginger cat, a ginger cat...Sounds familiar...Wait! There was a ginger cat hanging around my bakery just this morning. Is it the same cat?"

"It could be," said Simoux. "It's possible that the ginger cat you saw this morning and the ginger cat referred to in the sign are in fact the same animal. Thus, the animal in question encompasses both the signifier and the signified and so..."

"*Quoi?*" interrupted Jacques. "That's very complicated—remember, I'm not as smart as you are."

"My apologies, Jacques," said Simoux, patting him on the back. "All I meant was that it's probably the same cat."

"*Merci*, Simoux!"

The two men shook hands and Monsieur de Tutu set off for his bakery.

A ginger cat was sitting in front of the bakery—it was Baguette. Earlier that morning he had successfully traveled from the past into the present, but he hadn't gotten his destination quite right. He went from fourteenth-century France straight to present-day France instead of home—to present-day Moscow.

"*Bonjour, toujours!*" exclaimed Jacques when he saw the

cat. "My ginger friend, if you're the cat that the Petrov family has lost then I'll take you home immediately. After all, I'm a decent man. But you must give me a sign that it is indeed you. For instance, meow loudly three times. Yes, exactly three times—not two, not four, but three meows. That'll be the sign—an undeniable sign, a significant sign!"

I've never heard anything more ridiculous, thought Baguette, but he meowed exactly three times all the same.

"*Sacré bleu!* It is you! Please, come in!" said Jacques, excitedly opening the bakery door. "Please, have a croissant and then we'll be off. I'm a decent man and we can't waste another minute." Monsieur de Tutu gave Baguette a croissant, then put him in a bag, locked up his bakery, bought two plane tickets—one for a human and one for an animal—and the two of them flew 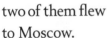 to Moscow.

CHAPTER 18

Lies

"He's back, Boss," said the Trash Man, bowing submissively before Noir. "Baguette is back."

"With the flower?" asked Noir impatiently.

"Without the flower, Boss. But with a Frenchman."

"A Frenchman?"

"Yes, he owns a bakery. His name is Jacques Saussure de Tutu. He found Baguette in France, put him in a bag and brought him here on a plane. At this very moment the Frenchman with a bag—more precisely, the Frenchman with Baguette in a bag—is heading to the Petrovs' apartment. He saw one of the 'Lost Cat' signs and is going to return the cat."

"Since Baguette doesn't have the flower, we don't need him," said Noir. "Leave the cat and the Frenchman alone. Sunset is less than an hour away—soon Purriana will be mine. I'll marry her and she'll give birth to black kittens. Kittens that are black as night, just like me."

"If I may, Boss, if I may disagree."

"What?!" said Noir, his fur standing on end. "You? Disagree? With me?"

"Yes, but only because I want to help you," quickly began the Trash Man. "You see, the Petrovs are offering a reward for the ginger cat, if you remember..."

"Of course I remember."

"Yes, Boss, your memory is superb, just like all your traits. The reward is a gold medal, one month's salary, a ring with an imitation diamond and an eternally green cactus...if you remember..."

"Yes, of course I remember," said Noir, becoming irritated.

"If you'll allow it, Boss, may I, that is to say, if you'll order me, may I take the bag with the cat away from the Frenchman? I'll pretend that I found the cat and the Petrovs will have to give me the reward. And I'll give it to you, Boss."

"I don't want their useless human junk!" laughed Noir. "I don't need their money, their diamonds or their gold. I'd take a juicy fish head over all that stuff any day."

"But, if I may, the cactus..."

"What?"

"The cactus."

"I don't need a cactus! What's gotten into you? Is your brain made of trash too? Take off that cap so I can have a look."

"As you wish, Boss," said the Trash Man. He lifted his cap, revealing a clump of dirty hair, then put it back on. "If I may, Purriana thinks the cactus is significant. I heard it with my

own ears—she said, 'Great-great-grandmother, your prediction wasn't wrong!'"

"Strange," said Noir thoughtfully. "There were rumors
going around about that cactus—the oracle was convinced
it could give cats nine lives, but she was wrong. She was
definitely wrong! The cactus was useless. Very strange...
What could've changed? What could've happened? Holy
claw!" he yelped suddenly. "Holy claw! I *need* that cactus!
Stop the Frenchman immediately! Have him smell this."
Noir handed the Trash Man a small vial with black powder.
"This vial contains a horrible poison—I made it from a unique
recipe using black magic. It's called nicatine. It's deadly for
cats but it only causes extreme drowsiness in humans. When
the Frenchman inhales it, he'll fall asleep for many years—
that's when you'll take his bag. Then go to the Petrovs and
say you found their cat. When they give you the reward
immediately come back here and above all guard the cactus
with your life!"

"Will do, Boss," said the Trash Man. He put the vial of
nicatine in his pocket and left the alley.

Monsieur Jacques Saussure de Tutu whistled as he walked.
Baguette was in the bag dangling from his shoulder. Monsieur
de Tutu was admiring the red evening sun. He was in such
a good mood that he stopped whistling and began to sing.

"*Oh, Champs-Élysées!*" he belted. "*Ohh, Champs-Élysées!*"

"If I may, it's impolite to sing so loudly in our city," said a passerby unexpectedly. Jacques stopped and looked at the passerby. He was wearing a dirty brown trench coat, an old cap with a rusted gold star and military boots that went up to his knees. His eyes were invisible behind the blurred lenses of huge horn-rimmed glasses.

"*Pardon,*" said Monsieur de Tutu, "*Je ne comprends pas* the language of Russian. You say how you love my song?"

"If I may," said the Trash Man, taking the vial out of his pocket.

"Oh, my friend, you want giving me a smelling of tasty tobacco?" With these words Monsieur de Tutu took the vial from the Trash Man's hands, brought it up to his nose and took a big sniff.

"*Merci,*" said Monsieur de Tutu and immediately fell asleep—his body sprawled out on the sidewalk.

"You're welcome," said the Trash Man. He took the bag with Baguette from the sleeping man and headed to the Petrovs' apartment. "Let's go, kitty. I'll take you to your mommy and daddy and they'll give me a reward!"

CHAPTER 19

The Cactus

"Where are you off to in such a rush, my kitty cat?" said Noir, blocking the way for Purriana.

"None of your business." Purriana tried to get around Noir, but he wouldn't let her pass.

"Sure it is, my striped darling," laughed Noir. "I'm your future husband. A wife should never keep any secrets from her husband!"

"You aren't my husband," hissed Purriana.

"Oh, yes, I am! Your former fiancé—your ginger Baguette— didn't bring back the flower. At sunset your great-great-grandmother will die and you'll marry me and give birth to black kittens!"

"There's still half an hour until the sun sets," said Purriana.

"Yes, but it doesn't matter. I know where you're going. You're going to the Petrovs'. To get the cactus."

"You know about the cactus?"

"I'm not stupid, you know," said Noir. "No, your

husband-to-be isn't stupid. I just saw it on Polina's window-sill. The cactus has flowered, hasn't it? When they found a flowerless cactus in the spot the oracle had described, every-one assumed that she had been wrong. But now a snow-white flower has bloomed on it. A Catlantic flower."

"Yes! So let me go! I'll tell Baguette about the flowering cactus—I heard he's back. He'll pick the flower and bring it to my great-great-grandmother. If he does it right away, he'll make it before sunset. Let me through, Noir! Please! The flowering cactus will give all of us nine lives!"

"Oh, no, my sweetheart, I can't do that," purred Noir. "I won't let you pass anywhere. My assistant, the Trash Man, has just gone to the Petrovs. He has returned Baguette and they've given him the promised reward: the salary, the gold medal, the ring with an imitation diamond and the cactus. By now the cactus is at my dumpster. I haven't seen it or smelled it yet but I was just about to…"

"Give me that cactus!" begged Purriana.

"Why would I do that, my darling? So you can take it to your great-great-grandmother? No way! The cactus is mine—I'm the only one who'll smell it and who'll have nine lives. And I guess I'll let my children, who'll be as black as me, smell it too. And that's it. No one else can smell it! Your striped oracle will never see this cactus, she'll have nothing to show to the Council and she'll die in shame. And all the striped cats will marry black cats. You, for instance: you'll marry me…"

"No!" whispered Purriana. "NO! NO! NO!" She began yelling in desperation, "Baguette! Save me, Baguette! SAAAAVE MEEE! Noir's tricked us! He has the flow—"

"Stop yelling," said Noir, irritated. He held Purriana's mouth shut with his black paw. "Be quiet, my darling. I think I'll marry you right now…"

CHAPTER 20

The Jump

Baguette was lying in the open porthole of the Petrovs' window on the twelfth floor. His ginger tail hung inside the room, his whiskers poked outdoors and his downy belly was suspended in the six-inch gap between the two window panes. So he wouldn't fall out, all twenty of his claws dug tightly into the window frame.

Everyone in the Petrov family was happy to have Baguette back, but Baguette was despondent. He had returned empty-handed. He hadn't accomplished the heroic feat in honor of his beloved. He hadn't found the Catlantic flower. At sunset his beloved Purriana would marry the black cat Noir.

My life is in shambles! thought Baguette. *Maybe I should just jump out of this twelfth-floor window?*

"Cheer up! Eat some salami," said Mama Petrov, holding out a piece for him. Baguette sniffed the salami then turned away, dejected. He had no appetite.

"Chew on this, friend." Bonehead offered Baguette his very favorite bone. "Chewing always helps—helps you forget."

"I don't want to forget," Baguette shook his head sadly. "I've already forgotten what the Catlantic flower looks like. I couldn't accomplish the feat—I'll remember this failure forever."

"Smell this flower," said Polina, holding a vase under his nose. "Look how beautiful it is. And it smells so wonderful. It'll cheer you up right away!" Baguette sniffed the flower and dismissively turned away. *How can I enjoy stupid, ordinary, human flowers when I'll never inhale the wonderful aroma of a Catlantic flower again?*

"Save me, Baguette! SAAAAVE MEEE!" came a cat cry from outside. Baguette jumped up and looked out the window—he recognized the voice of his beloved Purriana. He saw two cats on the street down below: Purriana and Noir. Noir was holding her tightly, covering her mouth with his black paw. Purriana was struggling, trying to escape.

"Let her go, you scoundrel!" yelled Baguette from his window.

"Never! She's mine now!"

"Let her go!" Baguette arched his back in fury.

"What're you going to do about it, ginger?" Noir looked up at the twelfth floor with a sneer. "What're you going to do? Jump down here?"

"I'll jump all right," whispered Baguette. Then he yelled, "I'm coming, my darling!" Baguette stood up in the open porthole, preparing to jump.

"Don't do it, friend!" whined Bonehead. "It's too high up—you'll kill yourself."

"Don't jump, Baguette!" yelled Purriana. "Don't jump from the twelfth floor—you'll never make it."

"I have no other choice," said Baguette quietly. "It's a question of honor—and honor is greater than life."

And Baguette...

And Baguette jumped.

"**M**ama, Mamaaa!" Polina ran into the kitchen, sobbing. "Our kitty cat! Our kitty jumped out the window! He's down there on the asphalt! He's dead!" The whole Petrov family gathered solemnly at the window. In the setting rays of the sun they could see something down below on the gray asphalt—a bright ginger splotch. The splotch was Baguette.

"Bowwww-wowwww!" howled Bonehead.

"Oh dear," whispered Papa. "Polina, don't look down there." Down below, a crowd was gathering around the motionless ginger cat.

"Oh, no! The Petrovs' kitty fell out of the window," said a neighbor. "He was probably hunting for birds."

"Ay, ay, ay, that poor cat," her husband shook his head. "What negligent owners! Why didn't they put a screen on their window? Or bars?"

"What an idiot," hissed Noir. "Jumping from that kind of height—he deserves it."

"Be quiet!" scolded a large white cat called Whale. "How can you speak ill of your own kind at a tragic time like this?"

"My darling Baguette!" sobbed Purriana, hugging his motionless body. "Why, Baguette? Why did you have to leave me this way?"

"May the ground feel like down feathers to him," said Whale quietly.

"Actually, the ground is quite hard," muttered Baguette, opening one eye. "Purriana, my Wonderful Cat, why would you think that I've decided to leave you?" And he opened his second eye.

"You're alive?!" said Purriana excitedly. "You're alive!" And she rubbed her soft pink nose against Baguette's strong masculine nose.

"He's alive," confirmed Whale happily.

"He is indeed," said Noir, his brow furrowed. "How very strange."

"Yes, I'm alive," said Baguette. "I jumped, I fell and then everything kind of...sort of...turned off. And then I saw a white cat."

"Me?" asked Whale.

"No, not you. This cat had wings."

"A cat with wings?!"

"Yes, with wings. White wings—like a chicken before it's been plucked. And this winged cat said to me, 'Ginger Baguette, your life has ended. This was your first life, now begins your second life. I wish you all the best in your personal life.'"

"I think I understand!" said Purriana. "You must've acquired nine lives. Baguette, did you smell the flowering cactus before the Trash Man took it away?"

"No, I didn't smell the cactus," said Baguette. "I smelled its flower—but that was after that rude, stinky man left with the cactus."

"What do you mean—after?" said Purriana.

"Yes, what exactly do you mean—after?" shrieked Noir.

"Well, it's all very simple," said Baguette. He stood up and shook himself off. "The stinky man came to the Petrovs. I was in his bag. He asked for the reward: the medal, the salary, the ring and the cactus. So, Vadik got his medal, Papa put his salary in an envelope, Mama took the ring off her finger and Polina went to get the cactus. She looked at the cactus for a long time. A couple of days ago a beautiful white flower had blossomed on it. And Polina said to me, 'I promised to give away my eternally green cactus for you, my dear Baguette. That's exactly what the sign said: "eternally green cactus." But there was nothing about a flowering cactus—the sign didn't say that. So I'm going to keep the flower. I hope you won't think I'm greedy, Baguette. For you, I'd give anything, it's just...the man who brought you is so stinky! He probably lives by the dumpster—the flower won't survive there. And this flower is very rare. I read in Vadik's encyclopedia that cactuses like this one only flower once every thousand years.' So Polina cut off the flower and put it in a vase. Then she gave the cactus to the stinky man."

"Is it still in the vase?" said Purriana in a quivering voice.

"What? The stinky man?"

"No! The flower! The Catlantic flower! Is it still in the vase?"

"Wait, so it's..." Baguette shut his eyes in concentration and suddenly remembered what the Catlantic flower looked like: it looked exactly like the flower in the vase. "Holy claw! It's a Catlantic flower! Yes, it's at our house in a vase. We have to bring it to the oracle right away. There's still a few minutes before sunset! Hey, Bonehead!" he yelled with all his might.

"You're alive, my friend!" barked Bonehead from the window.

"Yes, I'm alive. I need your help! Get the pretty white flower that's in the vase and throw it down!"

"Throw it down? Why? The Petrovs will scold me!"

"Do it for me, friend!"

"OK. For you, I'll do it." Bonehead grabbed the white flower with his teeth and threw it out of the window.

CHAPTER 21

Short and Sweet

The striped oracle was lying in her rocking chair. Her eyes were closed. The last ray of the sun was slowly disappearing from the attic. The members of the wise Council of Six were respectfully sitting around the chair.

"When did you say you were going to pass?" said the gray cat.

"Right after sunset," said the oracle in a feeble voice.

"There are only a few moments left," said the gray cat. "While you're still with us, on behalf of the Council, I must state our resolution. The wise Council of Six has determined: the striped oracle, who resides in the attic, has made two wrong predictions. First, she incorrectly predicted that the Catlantic flower would be at the florist's—instead of a flower it was a cactus. Then she predicted that the Catlantic flower would be brought to her by a ginger cat whose name begins with the letter 'B' and ends with the letter 'E,' and that he'd do so before she passed away—that is, before today's sunset.

As we can all see, the sun has almost set"—the gray cat pointed to the window with his paw—"and there is no sign of the ginger cat or the Catlantic flower. In the name of the Council of Six, we condemn the breed of striped oracles to disappear from the face of the earth. This evening every striped cat must marry a black cat and give birth to black—"

"Wait!" came Baguette's voice. "Wait! I have the flower!" Breathing heavily, Baguette and Purriana ran into the attic. Baguette held the white Catlantic flower in front of the oracle's face. In the setting sun's rays it looked crimson.

"Thank you, courageous Baguette," whispered the oracle barely audibly. "You've made my last moment a happy one."

"The Catlantic flower!" exclaimed the Council of Six. "Look! He's brought the Catlantic flower!"

The very last ray of sunlight disappeared—the sun had set.

"Farewell," said the oracle. She inhaled deeply, opened her eyes for just an instant, and went limp in her chair.

"Farewell, Great-great-grandmother!" Purriana began to weep.

"It's a bit early for farewells," said Baguette calmly. "She just smelled the Catlantic flower. She has eight long lives ahead of her."

The striped oracle sneezed and began to move in her chair.

"Excuse me," she said, "I must've dozed off…"

CHAPTER 22

More of an Afterword

Baguette and Purriana were married that very evening. All of the neighborhood cats came to their wedding with the exception of Noir, who stayed at his dumpster and scowled. The striped oracle danced at her great-great-granddaughter's wedding as if she were a teenage cat, and when she returned to her attic it was in the company of a very respectable gray suitor.

After the wedding, Baguette brought his new wife to the Petrovs' apartment (the newlyweds were planning on living there) and introduced her to the whole family. Polina, her older brother Vadik and Bonehead were all very excited to have a new cat. Mama and Papa were a little less excited, but they didn't protest—they respected their cat and his choice of wife.

As for the kind Frenchman, Monsieur Jacques Saussure de Tutu—he, unfortunately, remained asleep on the sidewalk for three whole days until Baguette, who was preoccupied with his new married life, finally remembered about him. But as soon as he remembered, the cat immediately took it upon himself to save Jacques. Baguette asked the white cat Whale for help. Whale used white magic to concoct an antidote for the awful nicatine. The antidote was called catine. A vial of the white aromatic catine was given to Bonehead, who, during his next morning walk, slyly put it under the Frenchman's nose.

"*Oh, mon Dieu! Quelle heure est-il, s'il vous plaît?*" mumbled the Frenchman as he awoke.

"How sad," said Papa Petrov, walking past him. "Look what can happen to a decent person! He certainly picked his poison."

How does Papa know about the poison? thought Bonehead, sniffing at the man's hands, which still smelled of croissants.

"No! Bonehead, don't touch him!" scolded Papa. "Sir, do you need some help?"

"*Oh, merci! Un grand merci. Pourquoi pas?*" said Jacques.

"He's not making any sense, the poor man's really out of it," said Papa. "I'll call an ambulance—they'll take care of him." Fifteen minutes later an ambulance took Monsieur de Tutu to the hospital. When he was discharged from the hospital a package was waiting for him. Inside he found the reward: a gold medal, a ring with an imitation diamond, one month's salary and an eternally green cactus. The wise Council of Six determined that the reward ought to be taken away from Noir and the Trash Man and given to the man who actually found Baguette—that is to say, to Monsieur Jacques Saussure de Tutu.

When he had gotten the package, Monsieur de Tutu went straight to the Petrovs. The thing is, Monsieur de Tutu was a decent man and had brought Baguette back from France because it was the right thing to do. He didn't need a reward for his good deed, so he returned almost everything to the Petrovs. He gave the gold medal back to Vadik, he gave the ring back to Mama and he gave the eternally green cactus back to Polina. The only thing he kept was Papa's salary. Of course, Monsieur de Tutu would've liked to return that as well, but he really needed the money to buy a return ticket to France. Somehow his wallet had mysteriously disappeared while he'd been asleep on the sidewalk for three days.

On his way to the airport Jacques noticed the black cat Noir. Noir hissed at him, his round yellow eyes glistening with hate. Noir was sure that Jacques would immediately run away in fear—since there's an omen that says black cats bring bad luck. But Monsieur de Tutu wasn't the least bit scared.

"Oh! A black cat!" exclaimed Jacques, reaching for Noir. "What luck! Come here, kitty-kitty!" Noir narrowly escaped Jacques's croissant-smelling hands and hid underneath the dumpster in panic. He watched as the strange Frenchman walked around, repeating to himself, "Wow, what luck! To see a purely black cat! I've dreamt about this my whole life!"

His strange behavior had a simple explanation: the French have very different omens. According to the French, black cats don't bring bad luck. On the contrary, they bring incredibly good luck to anyone who happens to see them.

On that fateful day, when the Frenchman was so happy to see Noir, things began to change. The bad omen about black cats began to lose its power—and Noir, his influence. He was no longer the self-appointed boss of all the dumpsters and no one was scared of him anymore—people calmly threw out their trash in the alley and didn't pay him any attention. And if they did pay him attention, it was only to scratch him behind his ears. Noir wasn't used to such nice treatment; he began molting, he lost his appetite and slimmed down. Soon, he left the alley, evidently in search of another, more suitable dumpster—one that was near people who didn't know that black cats weren't so bad after all. He wasn't seen around ever again.

About the Trash Man—left without a master, he got bored, became lazy, gained a lot of weight, stopped looking after himself and eventually turned into a giant pile of trash. He was taken away by the garbage truck one day, along with all the other trash.

And finally—after Baguette's big jump, Mama Petrov insisted that the window be fitted with bars. Papa installed the bars a few months later, but neither Baguette nor his wife Purriana were upset. On the contrary, they were happy with the decision. By that time Purriana had given birth to six beautiful striped ginger kittens, and there's nothing more dangerous for naive kittens than an open window on the twelfth floor.

"Safety first!" said Mama Petrov to Papa Petrov, looking proudly at the barred windows.

"I can rest easy now," said Mama Purriana to Papa Baguette.

And the kittens didn't say anything, because they couldn't talk yet.

ANNA STAROBINETS is an acclaimed, award-winning Russian novelist, screenwriter, and journalist. Best known as a writer of dystopian and metaphysical novels and short stories, she is also a successful children's author. *Catlantis* is her first children's book to be translated into English.

ANDRZEJ KLIMOWSKI studied at Saint Martin's School of Art and the Warsaw Academy of Fine Arts. He is an author of graphic novels and a designer of film and theater posters as well as numerous book covers, including the entire Everyman Collection of P. G. Wodehouse. He is a professor of illustration at the Royal College of Art.

JANE BUGAEVA was born in Russia and emigrated with her family to the United States at the age of six. She translates children's literature from the Russian and lives in North Carolina with her husband and two cats.

SELECTED TITLES IN THE
NEW YORK REVIEW CHILDREN'S COLLECTION

ESTHER AVERILL
Captains of the City Streets
The Hotel Cat
Jenny and the Cat Club
Jenny Goes to Sea
Jenny's Birthday Book
Jenny's Moonlight Adventure
The School for Cats

JAMES CLOYD BOWMAN
Pecos Bill: The Greatest Cowboy of All Time

PALMER BROWN
Beyond the Pawpaw Trees
Cheerful
Hickory
The Silver Nutmeg
Something for Christmas

SHEILA BURNFORD
Bel Ria: Dog of War

DINO BUZZATI
The Bears' Famous Invasion of Sicily

MARY CHASE
Loretta Mason Potts

VICTORIA CHESS and EDWARD GOREY
Fletcher and Zenobia

CARLO COLLODI and FULVIO TESTA
Pinocchio

INGRI and EDGAR PARIN D'AULAIRE
D'Aulaires' Book of Animals
D'Aulaires' Book of Norse Myths
D'Aulaires' Book of Trolls
Foxie: The Singing Dog
The Terrible Troll-Bird
Too Big
The Two Cars

EILÍS DILLON
The Island of Horses
The Lost Island

ROGER DUVOISIN
Donkey-donkey

ELEANOR FARJEON
The Little Bookroom

PENELOPE FARMER
Charlotte Sometimes

PAUL GALLICO
The Abandoned

LEON GARFIELD
The Complete Bostock and Harris
Leon Garfield's Shakespeare Stories
Smith: The Story of a Pickpocket

RUMER GODDEN
An Episode of Sparrows
The Mousewife

MARIA GRIPE and HARALD GRIPE
The Glassblower's Children

LUCRETIA P. HALE
The Peterkin Papers

RUSSELL and LILLIAN HOBAN
The Sorely Trying Day

RUSSELL HOBAN and QUENTIN BLAKE
The Marzipan Pig

RUTH KRAUSS and MARC SIMONT
The Backward Day

DOROTHY KUNHARDT
Junket Is Nice
Now Open the Box

MUNRO LEAF and ROBERT LAWSON
Wee Gillis

RHODA LEVINE and EVERETT AISON
Arthur

RHODA LEVINE and EDWARD GOREY
He Was There from the Day We Moved In
Three Ladies Beside the Sea

RHODA LEVINE and KARLA KUSKIN
Harrison Loved His Umbrella

BETTY JEAN LIFTON and EIKOH HOSOE
Taka-chan and I

ASTRID LINDGREN
Mio, My Son
Seacrow Island

NORMAN LINDSAY
The Magic Pudding

ERIC LINKLATER
The Wind on the Moon

J. P. MARTIN
Uncle
Uncle Cleans Up

JOHN MASEFIELD
The Box of Delights
The Midnight Folk

WILLIAM McCLEERY and WARREN CHAPPELL
Wolf Story

JEAN MERRILL and RONNI SOLBERT
The Elephant Who Liked to Smash Small Cars
The Pushcart War

E. NESBIT
The House of Arden

ALFRED OLLIVANT'S
Bob, Son of Battle: The Last Gray Dog of Kenmuir
A New Version by LYDIA DAVIS

DANIEL PINKWATER
Lizard Music

OTFRIED PREUSSLER
Krabat & the Sorcerer's Mill
The Little Water Sprite
The Little Witch
The Robber Hotzenplotz

VLADIMIR RADUNSKY and CHRIS RASCHKA
Alphabetabum

ALASTAIR REID and BOB GILL
Supposing…

ALASTAIR REID and BEN SHAHN
Ounce Dice Trice

BARBARA SLEIGH
Carbonel and Calidor
Carbonel: The King of the Cats
The Kingdom of Carbonel

E. C. SPYKMAN
Terrible, Horrible Edie

ANNA STAROBINETS
Catlantis

FRANK TASHLIN
The Bear That Wasn't

VAL TEAL and ROBERT LAWSON
The Little Woman Wanted Noise

JAMES THURBER
The 13 Clocks
The Wonderful O

ALISON UTTLEY
A Traveller in Time

T. H. WHITE
Mistress Masham's Repose

MARJORIE WINSLOW and ERIK BLEGVAD
Mud Pies and Other Recipes

REINER ZIMNIK
The Bear and the People